"Actually, I think I'll try a pint of Wild Horse tonight."

She moved the mug to the appropriate tap and tilted it under the spout. "Eleven whole words," she remarked. "I think that's a new record, John."

He lifted his gaze to hers, saw the teasing light in her eyes and felt that uncomfortable tug again. "My name's not John."

"But as you haven't told me what it is, I can only guess," she said.

"So you decided on John...as in John Doe?" he surmised.

She nodded. "And I think that's a smile tugging at the lips of the sullen stranger."

"I was just thinking that next time I'll order a Ruby Mountain Angel Creek Amber Ale," he said.

"Careful," she cautioned with a playful wink. "This exchange of words is starting to resemble an actual conversation."

He lifted the mug to his mouth, and Sky moved down the bar to serve a couple of newcomers, leaving Jake alone with his beer.

Which was what he wanted, and yet, when she came back again, he heard himself say, "My name's Jake."

The sweet curve of her lips warmed something deep inside him.

* * *

MATCH MADE IN HAVEN:
Where gold rush meets gold bands!

Dear Reader,

Welcome back to Haven, Nevada!

A string of failed relationships has convinced Skylar Gilmore that happily-ever-after isn't likely to happen for her, so she's decided to remain single rather than risk her heart again. Now the part-time bartender, counselor for at-risk youth and women's shelter volunteer fills her days with work, family and friends. And that's enough for Sky—until the night a mysterious stranger walks into the bar...

Searching for a new purpose and direction after his discharge from the Marine Corps, Sergeant Jake Kelly packs his duffel bag, whistles for his dog and heads to Haven, Nevada. The scars on his body don't begin to tell the story of the tragedy that haunts him, and the isolated ranch he inherited from his uncle seems like the perfect place to wage his solitary battle with PTSD.

So what happens when a wounded warrior who only wants to be left alone meets a warmhearted cowgirl who always wants to help? After a few insistent nudges from an adorable yellow Lab, the unlikely pair just might discover renewed hope for a future—together.

I hope you enjoy Sky and Jake's story! And watch for my next book, *Meet Me Under the Mistletoe*, coming in November 2020.

All the best,

Brenda Harlen

The Marine's
Road Home

———

BRENDA HARLEN

HARLEQUIN
SPECIAL
EDITION

Recycling programs
for this product may
not exist in your area.

ISBN-13: 978-1-335-89472-4

The Marine's Road Home

Copyright © 2020 by Brenda Harlen

For questions and comments about the quality of this book, please contact us at CustomerService@Harlequin.com.

Harlequin Enterprises ULC
22 Adelaide St. West, 40th Floor
Toronto, Ontario M5H 4E3, Canada
www.Harlequin.com

Printed in U.S.A.

Brenda Harlen is a former attorney who once had the privilege of appearing before the Supreme Court of Canada. The practice of law taught her a lot about the world and reinforced her determination to become a writer—because in fiction, she could promise a happy ending! Now she is an award-winning, RITA® Award–nominated nationally bestselling author of more than thirty titles for Harlequin. You can keep up-to-date with Brenda on Facebook and Twitter, or through her website, brendaharlen.com.

Books by Brenda Harlen

Harlequin Special Edition

Match Made in Haven

The Sheriff's Nine-Month Surprise
Her Seven-Day Fiancé
Six Weeks to Catch a Cowboy
Claiming the Cowboy's Heart
Double Duty for the Cowboy
One Night with the Cowboy

Montana Mavericks: Six Brides for Six Brothers

Maverick Christmas Surprise

Montana Mavericks: The Lonelyhearts Ranch

Bring Me a Maverick for Christmas!

Montana Mavericks: The Great Family Roundup

The Maverick's Midnight Proposal

Visit the Author Profile page
at Harlequin.com for more titles.

This book is dedicated to all members
of the armed forces—and to those who love them.
#NeverForget

Chapter One

Everyone had a story to tell.

Skylar Gilmore knew it was true, even if a lot of those stories weren't exactly page turners. Still, she was always willing to listen and fascinated by the characters telling the tales at Diggers' Bar & Grill.

From her position behind the polished walnut bar, she heard the accounts of regulars, less frequent customers and even the occasional tourist. To each, she offered a sympathetic ear without censure or judgment. After all, it wasn't her job to counsel—at least not here.

And so it was that she knew Chase Hampton intended to propose to Megan Carmichael before he'd even bought the ring, and that Erica Rainville had decided to leave her husband of twelve years—not because he was having an affair with his secretary but because *she* was, and also that Bobby Tanner and Holly Kowalski had postponed their wedding plans because they were unable to agree on when—or even if—they'd have kids.

Bobby had been in the bar again tonight, lamenting the apparent impasse with his fiancée. Six years older than his bride-to-be, Bobby was eager to start a family. But Holly, the junior deputy in the sheriff's department, wanted to establish herself in her career before she took time off to have a baby. Of course, that led to another argument, as Bobby expected that she would give up her job in order to be a full-time mother to their children.

Sky had to bite her tongue when he told her that. It was the only way to not break her concrete rule about listening without judgment. She didn't disagree that a job in law enforcement could be dangerous. How could she when her sister was an attorney married to the local sheriff? Sky knew only too well that Kate suffered through nights when her husband was called away from home.

But Kate would be the first to say that marriage was a partnership, and though partners might not always agree, they should always support one another. Since Kate and Reid would be celebrating their third wedding anniversary in only a few months, Sky had to trust that her sister was more of an authority on the subject of marriage than she was.

So instead of telling Bobby that he had no right to be making career decisions for the woman he claimed to love, Sky only encouraged him to keep the lines of communication open. He promised to do that, then finished his beer, tipped her generously and headed home to his fiancée.

"Does everyone who sits at the bar spill their guts to you?" Kate had asked one night, after listening to Roger Greenway bemoan the emptiness of his life as he sipped his rum and coke.

Sky couldn't help but empathize with the divorced father who only saw his kids twice a month now that his ex had remarried and moved out of town with them.

"Everyone," she'd confirmed in response to her sister's question.

Because it had seemed true at the time.

Before she'd met the handsome—and mysterious—stranger she referred to as John. In the six years that she'd been pouring drinks at Diggers', he was the lone holdout.

She'd been chatting with Jerry Tate when the newcomer walked into the bar around 9:50 p.m. on a Wednesday night five weeks earlier. But she'd caught a glimpse of him out of the corner of her eye, as he'd paused inside the door and surveyed the room—as if he was looking for someone.

Just over six feet tall, he had broad shoulders that tested the seams of his long-sleeved Henley-style shirt, and muscular legs encased in jeans faded almost white at the stress points. The simple attire did nothing to disguise his strength, and she was helpless to prevent the quiver that reverberated through her system.

And then his eyes had caught and held hers.

She'd started to smile, because she was a friendly person and because it had been a long time since she'd felt such an instantaneous awareness and intense attraction. But he clearly hadn't registered a similar reaction on his end, because he quickly shifted his gaze.

After scanning the room, he squared those wide shoulders and moved resolutely toward the bar. His pace was deliberate, unhurried, and as he drew nearer, Sky noted that his square jaw was unshaven and his eyes were the color of premium whiskey.

Despite the sting of his visual dismissal, Sky curved her lips again as the stranger edged a hip onto a stool at the bar. "Hi there."

His only response was a stiff nod of acknowledgment.

"New to town or just passing through?" she wondered aloud, as he perused the labels on the taps in front of him.

"I'll have a pint of Sam Adams."

A New Englander, she guessed, as she selected a glass mug and tipped it under the spout. There'd been no hint of an accent in his voice, but his chosen beverage might be a clue.

She set the beer on a paper coaster in front of him.

No "please" or "thank you," either, she noted, as he wrapped his hand around the mug.

"Are you from Massachusetts?" she asked.

"Or maybe New York?" she suggested as an alternative when he failed to reply, because New Yorkers had a reputation—deserved or not—for being standoffish and unfriendly.

Still no response.

"Rhode Island?" She grabbed that one out of thin air, hoping the random guess would get some kind of a reaction from him.

He lifted his gaze, and she felt another tug, low in her belly, when those whiskey-colored eyes locked on hers.

"I came in for a beer," he finally said. "Not company or conversation."

She was admittedly shocked by his blunt response.

And maybe a little hurt.

Because while he was certainly under no obligation to want company or conversation, she'd been a bartender long enough to know that people usually came into Diggers' seeking one or the other— or both. Those who only wanted a beer could just as easily crack one open under their own roof. Unless there was a reason they wanted to get away from home for a while, such as a nagging spouse or screaming kids.

The Sam Adams–drinking stranger had no ring on his finger and no tan line indicating that one might have recently been removed. Of course, Sky knew from experience that the lack of a wedding band wasn't necessarily indicative of anything.

Since his remark didn't invite any kind of response, she merely nodded and made her way to the other end of the bar to refill Ellis Hagen's empty glass.

As Sky poured another shot of Jack Daniels over ice, Ellis was happy to chat—even engaging in a little harmless flirting that soothed her inexplicably bruised feelings. And because she refused to let the rudeness of a stranger bring down her mood, Sky allowed herself to flirt back.

Of course, it was easy with Ellis, because they'd dated for a while way back in high school. In fact, she'd lost her virginity in the back seat of his Cavalier after the homecoming dance in her junior year. It had been a mostly forgettable experience for both of them, but he was the first boy she'd ever imagined herself in love with, and she was always happy to see him at the bar and catch up.

Tonight she was grateful, too, as her conversation with Ellis succeeded in taking her mind off the mysterious stranger so that she barely even noticed when he finished his beer and tucked a ten-dollar bill beneath the edge of his glass before walking out again without even a backward glance.

"Who's the new guy?" Courtney Morgan, one of the bar's waitresses, asked Sky.

"I don't know," she admitted, cashing out his tab and dropping his change into the tip jar.

Courtney seemed taken aback by her response. "A quiet one, is he?"

Sky nodded, though she suspected he was more than quiet.

He was a man with secrets—and she wanted to know all of them.

But she pushed him out of her mind, mostly, until the following Wednesday.

The bar was busier than usual that night, because Duke's Diggers—the coed softball team sponsored by the bar's owner—had played a rescheduled game, after which they came into the bar for the free wings that were a perk of playing for Duke.

"We missed you out there tonight," Caleb said to Sky.

He was the team's left fielder—and also the younger of her two brothers, married to his high school sweetheart and now father to an adorable two-week-old baby boy.

"You should have thought about that before you scheduled the game for a Wednesday night," she said, tipping a second pitcher beneath the tap. "How badly did we lose?"

"It wasn't bad at all," he said. "Only two runs. And they never would have got those two runs if you'd been on third."

"I appreciate your confidence, but it's a team sport," she reminded him.

"And the whole team—even Doug, who filled in at third—wished you could have been there."

She turned the pitchers of beer so that the handles were facing him. "Go drown your sorrows."

He shook his head even as he picked up the pitchers. "I promised Brie I'd head straight home after one beer."

"Look at you—a responsible husband and father," she remarked teasingly.

"I'm trying," he said. "It would be a lot easier if Colton would sleep more than three hours at a time."

"No one ever said parenthood was easy." But she could see the fatigue in the shadows under his eyes and felt a stirring of sympathy. "You want me to put in a separate order of wings to go for you?"

He nodded. "Honey hot."

Though not a flavor listed on the menu, Caleb liked his wings hot and Brielle liked honey garlic, so they compromised by getting them tossed in both sauces.

"You gonna share those pitchers of beer, Gilmore?" Chase Hampton called out from the round table in the corner.

"That's my cue," he said and headed off to join his teammates.

Sky had just sent the wing request through to the kitchen when the mysterious drinker of Sam Adams walked into the bar.

And damn, if he wasn't even better looking than she'd remembered.

She glanced at the clock—9:48 p.m.—and wondered if the timing of his appearance was a coincidence or if it was going to become a habit. And while she told herself she wasn't the least bit interested, she couldn't deny that she was curious.

He took the same seat at the bar, gave the row of taps a similar perusal. "I'll have a pint of Sam Adams," he said.

She poured the beer and set it in front of him.

Raucous laughter broke out at the table in the corner and his hand tightened around the mug, gripping it so hard his knuckles went white.

"That's our softball team," she told him, not sure why she was bothering to explain. "Tuesdays and Saturdays are the usual game days, but the rain last week forced the reschedule tonight."

He didn't respond.

Of course not, because he only wanted a beer, not company or conversation.

So she made her way down the bar, clearing away empty glasses and wiping the counter. The stranger finished his beer, put ten dollars beneath his empty glass and walked out again.

For three weeks after that, his routine was the same.

Every Wednesday night, just before ten o'clock, he came into the bar. Sometimes he was a few minutes earlier, sometimes a few minutes later, but it was always and only on Wednesdays.

He ordered one beer, drank the beer, left a ten-dollar bill on the bar and walked out again.

His routine was always the same.

He never came in with anyone.

He never left with anyone.

He never talked to anyone.

And after five weeks, Sky still didn't even know his name.

Sure, there were other ways she might have uncovered some information about him. Haven was a small enough town that she felt confident somebody knew something about the handsome stranger. But she wasn't interested in gossip and she didn't want secondhand information. She wanted *him* to tell her the secrets she sensed he'd buried deep inside—more important, she wanted him to *want* to open up to her.

But she'd settle for his name to start.

A few years earlier, after yet another failed relationship, Sky had decided that she was done with dating. Since then, she hadn't met a single man who tempted her to change her mind—until *he* walked into Diggers' on that Wednesday night.

She glanced at the vintage beer clock on the wall as she poured a couple of pints for Carter Ford and Kevin Dawson.

9:52 p.m.

And here come the butterflies.

Jake Kelly slid behind the wheel of his truck, turned the key in the ignition and shifted into gear. Even as he turned onto Main Street, he wondered, *what the hell am I doing?*

For the past two years, he'd focused his efforts on putting the past behind him and moving on with his life. He wasn't trying to forget—he didn't ever want to forget—but he knew that if he couldn't slay his demons, he had to find a way to coexist with them.

"You can't live like a hermit forever," Luke had said, when he visited Haven a few weeks back.

"No one lives forever," Jake had pointed out.

He'd thought the response might make his brother

crack a smile. Instead, the furrow between Luke's brows had only deepened, and he'd spent the next hour trying to get Jake to open up about his emotions, as if talking—especially to a man who couldn't possibly understand feelings of inadequacy and failure—was going to make anything better.

But Jake did promise that he'd make an effort to get out of the house more, to engage in social interaction and meet people. Which was how he'd ended up at Diggers' Bar & Grill that first Wednesday night in early May.

It had been a test, and though he wasn't entirely sure when he left the bar again whether he'd passed or failed, he'd at least had the satisfaction of knowing that he'd completed it. The next week, it was a little bit easier. And the week after that, easier still.

By the fifth week, he was thinking that he might be ready for a bigger challenge—and when he left the community center, he'd intended to head straight home. Yet for some inexplicable reason, he found himself driving toward Diggers' instead.

Or maybe the reason wasn't so inexplicable.

Maybe the reason was as simple—and complicated—as the incredibly appealing woman who worked behind the bar.

Her name was Skylar Gilmore, but most of the regulars referred to her simply as Sky. She had long dark hair that she usually wore tied back in a loose ponytail and eyes that were a unique mix of gray and blue, not unlike a stormy sky, outlined by a sweep of ridiculously long lashes. Her brows were delicately arched, her cheekbones high and sharp and her mouth looked as if it was meant to be kissed.

The unwelcome observation made him scowl.

She was about average height, but there was absolutely nothing average about her curves, shown to advantage by the scoop-necked white T-shirt that hugged the swell of her breasts and the slim-fitting black jeans that molded to her sweetly rounded bottom and long, shapely legs.

The first time he saw her, he'd felt a stir of something low in his belly. It wasn't a familiar or comfortable feeling. But maybe that was because, for the better part of two years, he'd focused on tamping down his emotions so that he wouldn't have to feel pain or loss or longing.

So yes, it had taken Jake a moment to recognize the feeling as attraction, and less than that to dismiss it. Not only because it was uncomfortable and unfamiliar, but because he wasn't foolish enough to let the attraction lead to anything else. He had no intention of making a move on the pretty bartender, because he knew no woman would want to deal with the issues that he was only beginning to deal with himself. And anyway, he had no wish to open himself up to rejection again.

But Sky greeted him tonight, as she always did, with an easy smile.

He didn't smile back.

He had no reason or desire to encourage her.

"Pint of Sam Adams?" she prompted, when he remained silent, scowling at the taps.

He only had to nod, and the beer would be poured and set in front of him. Instead, he heard himself say, "Actually, I think I'll try a pint of Wild Horse tonight."

She moved the mug to the appropriate tap and tilted it under the spout. "Eleven whole words," she remarked. "I think that's a new record, John."

He lifted his gaze to hers, saw the teasing light in her eyes, and felt that uncomfortable tug again. "My name's not John."

"But as you haven't told me what it is, I can only guess," she said.

"So you decided on John...as in John Doe?" he surmised.

She nodded. "And because it rolls off the tongue more easily than the-sullen-stranger-who-drinks-Sam-Adams, or, after tonight, the-sullen-stranger-who-usually-drinks-Sam-Adams-but-one-time-ordered-a-Wild-Horse." She set the mug on a paper coaster in front of him. "And I think that's a smile tugging at the lips of the sullen stranger."

"I was just thinking that next time I'll order a Ruby Mountain Angel Creek Amber Ale," Jake said.

"Careful," she cautioned, with a playful wink. "This exchange of words is starting to resemble an actual conversation."

He lifted the mug to his mouth and Sky moved down the bar to serve a couple of newcomers, leaving him alone with his beer.

Which was what he wanted...and yet, when she

came back again, he heard himself say, "My name's Jake."

The sweet curve of her lips warmed something deep inside him. "You got a last name, Jake?"

"Let's not rush into anything," he said. "We only just met."

She chuckled at that. "Maybe you'll tell me next week?"

"How do you know I'll be here next week?"

"Wild guess," she said.

"You really don't know my last name?"

"I didn't know your first name until a few seconds ago," she pointed out to him.

"And I thought there weren't any secrets in small towns."

"They are few and far between," she said. "But, in the interest of full disclosure, I will tell you that I know you're staying at Ross and Anna Ferguson's house."

"How do you know that?"

"The *G* in Circle G is for Gilmore," she said, naming the ranch property that was situated behind his uncle's land. "Which makes us neighbors."

He considered that as he tipped his glass to his lips and swallowed the last mouthful of beer.

"Well, maybe I will see you next week, neighbor," he decided aloud, as he took a ten-dollar bill out of his wallet and tucked it under the mug. "But right now, I need to get home. Molly's waiting for me."

Chapter Two

Who the heck was Molly?

Of course, Jake didn't stick around long enough for Sky to ask. And so the question continued to prod at the back of her mind throughout the following week.

The context of his remark suggested that Molly was his girlfriend. Or maybe even his wife. A possibility that sat uneasily with Sky—not just because she'd flirted with the man, but because he'd flirted back!

Or maybe she'd read too much into their brief conversation. Maybe the fact that his icy reserve had thawed enough to allow the exchange of a few words had been nothing more than that. In any event, she needed to get over her preoccupation with the man, because he was obviously involved with somebody else and she would never make a move on a guy who was taken.

"You're not going to get many tips with a scowl on your face," a familiar voice remarked teasingly.

Although Sky didn't keep any portion of the tips that were collected at the bar, she deliberately smoothed her brow and curved her lips for her brother-in-law.

"You're out late, Sheriff," she remarked.

"My wife decided that she had to have a spicy chicken wrap and curly fries."

Sky glanced pointedly at the clock. "At nine o'clock on a Wednesday night?"

He shrugged. "I've learned not to ask."

She keyed the order into the computer and sent it through to the kitchen. "Anything else?"

He shook his head. "I had pizza while I was finishing up some paperwork at the office."

"How about a beer while you're waiting?"

Now he nodded. "Yeah, that sounds good."

Sky poured a pint of Icky.

"So…how far along is she?" she asked, setting the mug in front of him.

Reid looked at her blankly. "Far along with what?"

"Maybe I'm wrong," she said. "But when was the last time Kate sent you out on an errand to satisfy her cravings?"

The blank expression on his face slowly gave way to realization. "When she was pregnant with Tessa."

Sky nodded.

"I don't… I can't…" he said, because apparently the possibility had inhibited his ability to form a complete sentence. "Do you really think…she might be pregnant?"

"You'd know the chances of that better than me," she said dryly.

He nodded, acknowledging the point, and lifted the mug of beer to his lips. "We haven't really been trying," he confided now. "I mean, we've been talking about it, but—"

"If you've only been talking, then I'm probably wrong," Sky teased.

Reid chuckled at that, though he still looked a little stunned by the possibility that his wife might be pregnant again. "As an only child, I often wished for a brother or sister," he admitted. "And since Tessa's first birthday, I've been dropping subtle hints about giving her a sibling."

"You only *think* your hints were subtle," she told him.

"And now… I can't believe it…it's finally going to happen."

"You might want to check with your wife before you start passing out cigars," Sky cautioned her brother-in-law. "I was only speculating about the possibility, based on her dinner request."

But now that she'd put the idea in the sheriff's head, he obviously wasn't ready to let it go. "You're right," he said. "I'm sure you're right. Katelyn's dinner order was a clue—and I didn't even pick up on it."

"Or maybe she's just messing with your mind," she suggested as an alternative.

"She wouldn't do that," Reid said.

"Instead of driving yourself crazy wondering, you could just ask her," she said.

He nodded. "I'll do that."

"And if she *is* pregnant, please don't tell her that I ruined the surprise."

"This conversation never happened," he promised. "So long as *you* tell *me* why you keep looking at the clock."

"Just counting the hours until the end of my shift," she said.

Now Reid shook his head. "You're waiting for someone."

"You should put your investigative talents to work in the sheriff's office—except that those in law enforcement generally require actual evidence before arriving at conclusions."

"Lucky for you, being a smart-ass isn't against the law."

She grinned. "And it's a lot better than being a dumbass."

Reid swallowed another mouthful of beer. "I heard Ross Ferguson's nephew has become something of a regular here," he remarked casually.

She wondered if he was changing the subject or if he'd somehow figured out that she was watching the clock in anticipation of Jake's arrival. Either way, she kept her response vague. "Did you?"

"Come on, Sky. Don't make me drag you down to the station for an interrogation."

"The bar isn't quite as sacred as the confessional, but there is an understanding between a bartender and her customers."

"Would you tell me if you'd had any trouble with him?"

"If it was the kind I didn't think I could handle on my own, yes," she said. "But Jake hasn't caused any problems at all."

Reid nodded then, accepting her response.

"Is there any reason you would suspect he might cause trouble?" she asked.

"No," the sheriff admitted. "It's just that he's been in town for a few months now and no one seems to know much about the guy."

"I didn't think that keeping to oneself was a crime in this town, either," she remarked.

"It's not a crime, but it is an anomaly." His cell phone vibrated against the bar and he turned it over to glance at the screen, his brow furrowing.

"Problem?" she asked.

"Another complaint about motorcycles driving recklessly on the highway," he said. "It's the third this month."

"You haven't made any arrests?"

"No one's been able to get even a partial license plate number," he confided. "And the descriptions of the alleged riders and their bikes have been anything but consistent."

"But you know who it is, don't you?"

"I have some suspicions, but without anything more than that—" He shrugged. "I just hope I get some proof before someone ends up seriously hurt... or worse."

Courtney brought a takeout bag from the kitchen and set it on the bar beside the sheriff. "Spicy chicken wrap and curly fries."

"Thanks."

The waitress smiled. "Give Katelyn my best."

"Will do," he promised.

As Reid pulled out his wallet, Sky glanced at the clock again.

9:53 p.m.

"It's Kelly," Jake said, after he'd taken his usual seat at the bar.

Sky wondered if he was picking up where their conversation had left off and, if so, she was a little confused because she'd been certain that "Molly" was the name he'd mentioned the previous week.

"My last name," he clarified, in response to her quizzical look.

"Jake Kelly," she said, trying it out. It was a strong name and suited the man. "So what can I get for you tonight, Jake Kelly?"

"That Wild Horse I had last week wasn't bad," he said.

"You should aspire to something a little better than not bad." She tapped a finger against the green label with the image of reptile bones. "There's a reason Icky is our most popular seller."

He shook his head. "I can't get my head around the idea of drinking a beer that goes by that name."

"It's named after Nevada's official state fossil," she told him.

"It's also the word my three-year-old niece uses to describe brussels sprouts."

"I share your niece's aversion to brussels sprouts," Sky said, tipping a glass beneath the tap to pour a sample. "And I promise you, Icky doesn't taste anything like green vegetables."

"I actually don't mind brussels sprouts," he said, but he still looked skeptical about the beer as he studied the light copper-colored liquid.

"Try it," Sky urged.

With a shrug, he lifted the glass to his lips.

"Well?" she prompted.

"Much better than the sprouts," he decided.

She selected a clean mug from the shelf and poured him a pint.

He reached for the glass before she'd pulled away, and his fingertips brushed over the back of her hand. She knew the contact was inadvertent—even before he yanked his hand away again—but that knowledge did nothing to alleviate the tingles that danced up her arm. And when she glanced at him, she could tell that he'd felt something, too, and that he was none too pleased about the fact.

Of course he wouldn't be, because there was another woman—though she still didn't know precisely what his relationship was with the mysterious Molly—waiting for him at home. And it really sucked for Sky that the first guy she'd experienced any chemistry with in a very long time was involved with somebody else.

"We also have a decent menu," Sky said, "if you ever wanted a bite along with your beer. Or if you wanted to bring Molly in to enjoy a meal."

"Molly?" he echoed blankly.

She hesitated, wondering if she'd made a mistake in mentioning the woman's name. Was he the type of guy who had a different girlfriend every week? Had he already moved on to someone new?

But since he was obviously waiting for an explanation of her remark, she said, "The woman you said you had to get home to last week."

"Oh, right." The hint of a smile tugged at one side of his mouth as he glanced around. "This really isn't her kind of place."

Sky wasn't offended by his remark. Though Diggers' did a good business as both a restaurant and a bar, she knew that the roadhouse-style establishment wasn't to everyone's liking and that its popularity had as much to do with the limited options in town as its menu offerings.

"We do a fair amount of takeout business, too," she said, offering him another option.

"I'll keep that in mind," he said.

She nodded and moved down the bar to serve another customer.

Because she wasn't the type of woman to make a move on another woman's man—but no other man had ever tempted her like Jake Kelly did.

* * *

Twelve weeks after he'd picked up the key from his uncle's lawyer, Jake was still adjusting to life in Haven, Nevada. Molly, on the other hand, had immediately and fully embraced the freedom of the countryside, and he suspected she would be less than thrilled when it was time to go back to San Diego.

Because they *would* have to go back, but not yet.

Not until he'd figured out what he was going to do with the rest of his life now that his military career was over.

It was a question he'd always known he would face one day. He'd just never expected that day to come before his thirtieth birthday. And now, two years later, he was no closer to finding the answer than he'd been when he got his discharge papers along with his purple heart.

"Molly!"

There was no response to his call, so Jake put his fingers in his mouth and whistled. He scanned the yard, looking for any sign of his canine companion, then whistled again.

Finally she appeared, bounding over the fence and racing toward him.

He sighed as she came to an abrupt halt in front of him, her tongue lolling out of her mouth, her big dark eyes shining with happiness.

"You've been trespassing again, haven't you? And probably chasing squirrels, too," he surmised.

Her attention deficit was probably the reason she'd flunked out of training to be certified as an emotional support animal, but the trainer's loss was Jake's gain. Molly had been his closest friend and confidante for more than two years now, and during that time, he'd never awakened from a nightmare alone. She might not always come right away when she was called, but she didn't need a certificate to know when someone was hurting.

"If the neighbors complain, I'm going to have to put up a real fence—or keep you on a leash," he warned her now.

Molly's tail waved in the air.

"And who's this?" Jake asked, as another creature emerged from under the lowest fence rail, apparently having followed Molly home. He dropped to his haunches and held out a hand for the miniature ball of fluff. "Hey there, little guy."

The pup sniffed his hand, then gave his finger a tentative lick, its little tail wagging its whole back end when Jake gently stroked the underside of its chin.

"She's a girl."

Jake glanced up to see another girl—this one of the human variety—climb over the fence.

Not a child but a teenager, he guessed. Maybe thirteen or fourteen, with blond hair tied back in a ponytail. She wore a Foo Fighters T-shirt over a pair of faded denim cutoffs with thong-style sandals on her feet to show off toenails that were each painted a different color.

"And—" the human girl continued, wagging her finger at the pup "—Rey is a very bad girl." Then she looked up at Jake again, offering a shrug and a smile. "We're still working on heel and stay. By the way, I'm Ashley Gilmore."

"Jake Kelly," he told her.

"You're Mr. Ferguson's nephew right? From California? I heard you'd moved in, but I haven't seen you around town," she continued, without giving him a chance to respond. "What do you think of Haven so far?"

"I haven't seen too much of it," he admitted.

She rolled her eyes. "There's not much to see."

He couldn't help but smile at that.

"What's your dog's name?" she asked now.

"Molly."

"She's a Lab?"

"Mostly."

"How old is she?" Ashley wanted to know.

"Almost three years."

"Rey's only three months."

He frowned. "I thought you said your dog was a girl."

"Not *R-A-Y* but *R-E-Y*, like the main character in the latest Star Wars trilogy," she explained. "I'm not a huge fan of the movies, but Rey had her name before I got her. Princess, her mom, was a pregnant stray who snuck into the horse stable at the Silver Star—that's my cousin Patrick's dude ranch—but she had trouble delivering her babies, so Patrick rushed her to the vet clinic in town and Brooke did an emergency C-section and her son Brendan named all the puppies after Star Wars characters and now

Patrick and Brooke are engaged. They haven't set a date for the wedding yet, but it probably won't be before Caleb and Brielle's wedding reception."

And then, before he could ask—or even decide if he wanted to know—she continued, "Caleb is my brother—well, my half brother, because we have the same dad but different moms. And Brielle is his wife, but she's also my cousin. They got married at the end of high school, but then Gramps literally had a coronary when he found out that his granddaughter had married a Gilmore."

"Do you mean literally in its true sense or are you using the new definition of the word?"

"I mean literally in its true sense," she assured him. "He almost died and had to have a triple bypass."

"So what was the big deal about—wait, didn't you say your name was Gilmore?"

She nodded. "It is now, but back then I was a Blake and Gramps had no idea that David Gilmore was my father. Probably because my mom knew that if she told him, her father would have a heart attack."

He was still trying to put together the pieces of information she'd revealed about her family.

"So are you related to Sky Gilmore?"

Ashley nodded. "Skylar's my sister. Half sister," she clarified again. Then her gaze narrowed. "How do you know Sky?"

"I don't really," he said. "But I've been into Diggers' a few times when she's been working behind the bar."

"Our dad hates that she works there."

"Why?"

"Because he didn't pay for a fancy college degree so that she could pour beer at the local watering hole," Ashley said.

He was curious to know what course of study had resulted in her fancy degree, but he didn't ask. He didn't want to appear to be taking too much of an interest in his uninvited visitor's sister.

"Anyway," the girl continued, "Brie blamed herself for Gramps ending up in the hospital, so she filed for divorce and moved to New York City to go to college but Caleb never signed the papers and now they're together again and they just had a baby a few weeks ago. His name is Colton and he's absolutely adorable."

"So your cousin's son is also your nephew," he said.

Her head bobbed again.

"It really is a small town, isn't it?" he mused.

"You have no idea," she told him, with such heartfelt emotion he had to fight against the smile that wanted to curve his lips. "I thought it was bad when me and my mom lived in town, but since we moved out to the ranch, it's even worse. I think they finally gave in and let me get a puppy because there is no one to hang out with and *nothing* to do."

"A dog can be good company," he agreed, certain that he wouldn't have made it through the past two-and-a-half years without Molly by his side.

"The instructor at obedience school said puppies should have the chance to play with other dogs, too, to learn social skills," she said. "And Rey really seems to like Molly."

He could hardly deny it. Not when Molly was sprawled on the grass and letting the puppy crawl over her.

"Is this her ball?" Ashley asked, picking up a tattered tennis ball.

"One of many," he admitted.

"Does she fetch?"

"She would fetch all day if someone was willing to throw for her."

"Maybe she could teach Rey how to fetch." Ashley drew back her arm and let the ball sail through the air.

Molly immediately took off after the projectile and Rey, startled by her canine pal's sudden abandonment, chased after her.

"You've got a pretty good arm," Jake noted.

"I'm gonna play on Diggers' softball team with my brother and sister someday," she said. "But I've gotta be eighteen before I can try out." Her wistful expression lifted when she saw Molly trotting back toward her.

The dog dropped the ball at Ashley's feet and sat, waiting patiently for the girl to throw it again.

Jake knew he should nudge his visitor along. He didn't want to gain a reputation for welcoming uninvited guests. But she was just a bored kid, happy to throw a ball for his dog, and since Molly was obviously happy, too, Jake saw no reason not to let Ashley stay a while longer.

Rey quickly tired out chasing after the bigger dog. When the tiny fluff ball collapsed by Jake's feet, he couldn't resist scooping her up. She snuggled contentedly in the crook of his arm, exhaled a weary sigh and promptly fell asleep.

Ashley glanced at the oversize face of her Apple Watch as Molly dropped the ball at her feet. "I have to go," she said, sounding sincerely regretful. "Exams start next week and my friend Chloe's coming over to study with me."

Jake nodded and exchanged the pup he held for the slobbery ball in Ashley's hand.

Molly looked at him expectantly, obviously wanting him to take over the game her new friend had abandoned.

"Done," he said firmly.

The dog looked at Ashley.

"Done," she echoed.

Resigned to the fact that playtime was over, Molly stretched out on the ground.

"Maybe I could bring Rey over to play with Molly again sometime?" Ashley suggested hopefully.

Jake sincerely doubted that he could stop her, and yet he felt compelled to caution. "I don't know that your parents would approve of you hanging out here."

"They won't mind, so long as they know where I am."

He wasn't entirely sure that was true, but he wasn't going to argue the point with her.

"So…can I?" she pressed.

"If you come by and Molly's in the backyard, I don't think she'd mind playing with Rey," he decided.

Ashley rewarded him with a radiant smile. "You know, socialization is important for people, too."

Though he didn't want to hurt her feelings, he felt he needed to be honest with her. "I'm not sure how long I'm going to be in town, but I wasn't planning on making friends while I was here."

The girl shrugged philosophically. "I've learned that sometimes the best things in life come along when we're not looking for them."

Chapter Three

On Saturday, Sky headed into town to Diggers' again. But this time, instead of work, she was there for lunch with Alyssa Channing.

The high school math and science teacher had moonlighted as a bartender a couple of years earlier, before falling in love with and marrying Jason Channing. Though Sky had only worked with her for a short while, they'd remained friends, even if Sky's various jobs and Alyssa's new roles as wife and mother made it challenging for them to get together.

After placing their orders, Sky scooped her friend's seven-month-old daughter out of her carrier and cuddled her close. "I can't believe how much Lucy's grown since I last saw her."

"You haven't seen her in almost three months," Alyssa pointed out. "And babies grow fast."

"Why do you sound sad?" Sky wondered.

"Because as fast as she's growing, she's still just a baby… I can't bear the thought of leaving her in the care of a stranger when I go back to work in September," her friend confided.

"It was hard for my sister, too," Sky told her. "There were several times, in the first few months, that Kate went to court with the baby strapped to her body."

Alyssa chuckled. "Unfortunately, I can't imagine my principal allowing that—especially not in the chemistry lab."

"I would guess not," Sky agreed, as her cell phone chimed with a message. She glanced at the screen, more out of habit than interest, because she had no intention of letting anything distract her from catching up with a friend she hadn't seen in far too long.

But worry dropped like a lead weight into the pit of her stomach when she recognized the number and read the brief words.

Can we talk?

"I'm sorry," she apologized to Alyssa. "I have to make a quick call."

"Of course," her friend immediately agreed, understanding the nature of Sky's job as a counselor required her to be available when her clients needed her—and that wasn't often during regular office hours.

Sky returned Lucy to her mama's arms and slipped away from the table, ducking into the alcove by the restrooms where it was a little quieter and she could give her full attention to the conversation with Jodie Dressler.

It had always been Sky's plan to work with kids struggling with grief, to help them cope. But to specialize in such a narrow field would have required her to move away from Haven to a much larger city. Maybe it was the loss of her own mother at a young age, exacerbated by the fear of losing her father, too, when he'd suffered a heart attack eighteen months earlier, that made her cling to the family she had left. Whatever the reason, she'd opted to stay in Haven and use her education and training to help wherever she could. Currently that entailed working a couple of days a week as a teen counselor at the local high school and being on call to counsel victims of abuse at a nearby women's shelter.

Sky had met Jodie at the local high school, where she had office hours two days a week. For the past few months, she'd been teaching the teen positive conflict resolution strategies to help with tension at home. And Jodie had been making good progress, until her mom decided to get back together with an old boyfriend, introducing a whole new source of friction into their already contentious relationship.

"What's going on?" she asked when Jodie answered the call.

Jodie's muffled sobs told Sky that the teen was sincerely distressed, and she struggled to piece together the few words that she could decipher through the girl's tears.

"Where are you now, Jodie?" she asked gently.

"I'm at the p-park…with Mason."

"The park by your house?"

"Uh-huh." She sniffled. "I d-didn't know where else to g-go."

But she'd gotten out of the house, away from her mother's boyfriend, Leon Franks, who was suddenly paying more attention to Jodie than her mom.

"Stay where you are," Sky instructed. "I'm on my way."

"Th-thank you."

Sky disconnected the call and returned to the table where she'd left her friend. "I'm sorry," she said again.

"Don't be. I already asked Deanna for a take-out container." Alyssa gestured to the compostable clamshell on the table beside the plated burger and fries. "When it wasn't a quick call, I figured you might have to go."

"You figured right," Sky said, reaching into her purse for her wallet.

Alyssa waved her away. "Go. I've got this."

"Next time it's on me," Sky promised, giving her friend a quick hug and dropping a kiss on top of Lucy's head.

After almost three years spent working with teenagers, Sky had mostly learned to distinguish between what was real and what was imagined. That wasn't to say that she didn't make mistakes or take missteps, but when she erred, it was always on the side of protecting a child.

She'd just pulled onto the highway when her low-fuel indicator dinged. She glanced at the display: 35 miles to empty.

Muttering a curse under her breath, she quickly calculated the length of her journey. She was headed in the opposite direction of the gas station, but it was less than fifteen miles to Jodie's house, and only a quarter mile more to the park where the girl had said she'd be waiting. She had more than enough gas to make it there and back again.

Of course, she hadn't anticipated that Jodie's mom's boyfriend might come looking for her, prompting the girl to leave the park with her boyfriend. Or that they'd drive to a local fast-food place another five miles away. They met there to figure out a plan of action and, after Mason left for his part-time job, Sky drove Jodie to her aunt's house, where she would spend the night. Though Leon Franks hadn't yet crossed any lines that warranted reporting, Jodie's discomfort around him was enough of a red flag for Sky that she decided to nudge her brother-in-law the sheriff to look into the man's background.

After the teen was settled, Sky finally turned back toward her own home. She eyed the low-fuel light warily but, based on her rough estimate, figured she still had enough left in her tank to get to the Pump & Go.

Eight miles from the gas station, Sky discovered that she was wrong.

Molly loved to ride in the truck, but she didn't love having to stay in the truck when Jake ran errands, so he usually left his canine companion at home when he went to do his weekly grocery shopping. Of course, she heard him swipe his keys off the counter and immediately lifted her head, a hopeful look in her big brown eyes.

"Didn't you have enough excitement making friends with Rey and playing fetch with Ashley today?"

Her ears perked up in response to the word *fetch*, but she didn't get too excited because she could see that he didn't have a ball in his hand.

"All right," he relented. "I should be quick today, so you can come along if you want."

Molly's tail thumped against the ground, more tentative than enthusiastic.

Chuckling to himself, he spoke the words he knew she'd understand. "Do you wanna go for a ride?"

She immediately sprang to her feet and made a beeline to the back door.

"I'll take that as a yes," he said.

Molly raced ahead of him to the truck.

When he opened the door, the dog immediately leaped onto the seat and took up her favorite position by the passenger window, her nose against the glass, her tail wagging.

Jake slid behind the wheel for the trip to Battle Mountain, lowering the passenger side window several inches for Molly.

There was a grocery store in Haven, of course, and he'd stopped in at The Trading Post a couple of times when he'd only needed to pick up one or two items. What he'd learned from those brief visits to the store was that that staff were overly friendly and chatty—not unlike Diggers' sexy bartender, though no one behind the deli counter or at the cash registers had stirred his interest the way Sky Gilmore did. In any event, those visits had cemented his resolve to get his supplies in Battle Mountain, where nobody knew his name or even cared who he was.

He'd just turned onto the highway when he spotted an SUV off to the side of the road with its hood up.

Actually, Molly had spotted the vehicle first and barked to draw his attention to it. She was always excited by the opportunity to meet new people.

Jake didn't want to stop. Besides, Haven being the kind of town where neighbors looked out for one another, he was fairly certain that if he continued on by, the next vehicle to come along would stop to offer assistance to the stranded driver. The battle between his desire not to get involved and his instinct to help someone in trouble was a short one.

"We've got groceries to buy," he reminded the dog, but his foot was already moving from the accelerator to the brake pedal. "And your favorite kibble is one of the items on my list."

Molly barked again—*at him* this time.

"You're supposed to be man's best friend, not my conscience," he grumbled, even as he pulled onto the gravel shoulder.

As he did so, the owner of the stalled Jeep Renegade stepped into view, and he realized it was none other than Sky Gilmore.

She wasn't dressed in her usual uniform of T-shirt and jeans today. Instead she was wearing a cropped sweater with a flowy skirt and chunky-heeled ankle boots, and he couldn't help but take notice of the long, shapely legs beneath the short hem and the sexily windblown hair that tumbled over her shoulders.

Wishing he could have ignored the dog and his own conscience, he nevertheless pushed the door open and, with a terse command to Molly to stay, stepped out onto the gravel.

Recognition widened Sky's eyes even as her lips curved. "Well, hello, neighbor."

Her slow, sexy smile took his breath away. Every. Single. Time. That unwelcome awareness churned in his belly, spread through his veins.

He shifted his gaze even as he took a few steps closer, to peer under the hood. "Engine trouble?" he asked.

"No," she admitted, a little sheepishly. "I ran out of gas."

"You think the gas tank is under the hood?"

She rolled her eyes. "A lot of people will drive by

a vehicle parked by the side of the road, but the hood up is a clear sign of trouble."

And running out of gas was a clear sign of carelessness, he thought, though he refrained from saying so aloud.

"Your SUV doesn't have a fuel gauge?" he asked instead.

"Of course it does."

"But no visible or audible indicators that your fuel is low?"

"Those, too," she admitted, a hint of color staining her pale cheeks.

"So how is it that your tank is empty?"

"I had enough gas to get me where I was going," she said, a little defensively. "But I had to make an unexpected detour, and then didn't have enough to get back again."

"And there were no service stations wherever you went?"

"If your only reason for stopping was to make snide comments, you can go," she said. "I was just about to call my brother to bring me a can of gas."

"I can't in good conscience leave you stranded on the side of the road," he said, turning back to his truck.

"I won't be here long," she assured him.

"And I'm just supposed to take your word for that?"

"You're not supposed to do anything," she said. "You were under no obligation to stop and you're under no obligation to stay."

Whether because she recognized the word *stay* or just wanted to meet his new friend, Molly barked, drawing Sky's attention.

"Quiet, Molly," he said.

The surprise on Sky's face shifted to curiosity as she turned to look toward his truck, where the retriever had her front paws curled over the edge of the lowered glass.

"So Molly's a dog," she mused.

"I never said any different," he said, perhaps a little defensively.

"No," she acknowledged. "But you had to know that I'd think otherwise."

"I can't control what people think," he said, all too aware that he'd been the subject of much speculation since his arrival in town.

"When a man mentions that a named female is waiting for him, it's reasonable to assume he's referring to a woman." She offered her hand for the dog to sniff. "A girlfriend or maybe even a wife." She rubbed the soft fur under the dog's throat, and chuckled when Molly closed her eyes and sighed blissfully.

"If I ever meet a woman as loyal as my dog, I might want to rush home to her," he remarked.

"Sounds like there's a story there."

He shrugged. "Only the same sad tale that's been told a thousand times before."

"Every story is unique," Sky insisted.

Even if that was true, Jake had no intention of sharing any details of his.

"Would I be correct then in assuming that you don't have a girlfriend or wife?"

"No girlfriend or wife," he confirmed. "But lucky for you, I do have a can of gas."

"Thank you," she said, when he retrieved the gas can from the bed of his truck. "I would have called one of my brothers—or even my father, but I'm sincerely grateful that I won't have to, because I'd never hear the end of it."

"No worries," Jake said, uncapping her gas tank and inserting the nozzle. "Though I should warn you, this might not solve your problem."

"What do you mean?"

"Fuel injectors can fail from overheating if they've been allowed to go dry, so putting gas into your tank might not be enough to get your vehicle started again."

"Of course not," she muttered under her breath. "Because no good deed goes unpunished."

The cryptic remark piqued his curiosity, but Jake didn't ask for an explanation. Instead, he focused on his task so they could both continue on their separate ways.

He tipped the gas can, his ears straining to identify a sound in the distance…

A trickle of sweat snaked down his spine, between his shoulder blades.

After six months in Afghanistan, he should be used to sweating by now. But this wasn't his body's futile effort to regulate its internal temperature when it was a hundred and twenty-five degrees outside. This was his body taking cues from his brain, telling him to be alert. To be ready.

Because anyone—from the twelve-year-old boy supposedly en route to visit his grandparents in the neighboring village to the seventy-year-old grandmother on her way to the open-air market—could be friend or foe. It wasn't just the twenty-something-year-old men with hard eyes who could be carrying weapons or wearing explosive devices.

And anyone who let down his guard, for even a second, could end up dead.

He focused on the sound, attempting to determine the direction of the bike's approach. Not a bike but bikes, *he realized. At least two—maybe three. He scanned the horizon, looking for the telltale cloud of sand kicked up by churning tires.*

There—he could see them now. Barely visible in the distance, but moving in their direction.

"Am I good to go now?"

It was Sky's voice—the distinctly feminine and familiar cadence—more than the question that drew Jake back.

He blinked, and the hazy, barren landscape faded away.

Not real.

He exhaled a long, slow breath.

But the motorcycles *were* real, because he could still hear the roar of the engines, approaching fast.

Not terrorists or insurgents, though. He didn't have to worry about ISIS or the Taliban in northern

Nevada. There was nothing to worry about here but his own overactive imagination.

"Jake?" Sky prompted.

"Yeah," he finally responded to her question as he recapped the gas can. "You're good to go."

She smiled then, and he felt that tug again. A distinctly sexual—and decidedly unwelcome—attraction.

"Thanks," she said.

He just nodded.

"Well—" she gave his dog one last affectionate scratch behind the ears "—it was nice to meet you, Molly."

The Lab dropped her chin to rest on the rolled down window as Sky turned away.

Jake felt a bead of sweat begin to snake down his spine for real as the sound of the engines grew louder.

Definitely more than one.

Not terrorists or insurgents, he reminded himself.

Probably just idiot kids racing.

His suspicion was confirmed when the first bike came into view around the bend with two more in close pursuit. All three took the curve wide, crossing to the wrong side of the center line, and going too fast to be able to correct their position.

"Look out!"

The urgency in Jake's tone had Sky's head whipping around.

She sucked in a breath as she spotted the trio of

motorcycles racing toward her. She had to get out of the way, to get off the road, but her feet were frozen, unable to move, even as the bikes drew closer.

Then Jake grabbed her arm and yanked her back, body-slamming her against the bed of his truck. The shock of the impact knocked the air out of her lungs. Her heart was racing; her head was spinning.

The bikes had seemed to appear from out of nowhere, and if Jake hadn't been there to warn her...

No, he hadn't just warned her, he'd saved her.

Or maybe that was a little melodramatic.

She didn't think any of them had passed too close to the spot where she'd been standing, but he'd immediately anticipated the danger and taken action. And she'd be lying to herself if she didn't admit that it was an incredible turn on.

Or maybe it was the press of his hard body against hers that was responsible for waking up her hormones. Because wrapped in his arms, how could she not be aware of him? The heat of his body? The scent of his skin?

And that awareness had her long-dormant hormones doing backflips, celebrating the fact that she wasn't just alive but cradled in the embrace of a strong, sexy man.

"Sky? Are you okay?" Jake loosened his hold and took half a step back, his gaze skimming over her as if assessing her for injury.

She licked her suddenly dry lips. "Yeah."

"You're shaking," he noted, rubbing his hands gently up and down her arms.

She nodded, because it was true. From the top of her head to the soles of her feet, her entire body was trembling. Not with fear, as he suspected, but with awareness and arousal.

"I'm okay," she said again.

While her brain warned her to push him away, her body was encouraging her to take a different tack. Urging her to lift herself onto her toes and press her mouth to his.

But her knees were still feeling a little wobbly, so she settled for leaning forward and pressing her lips to the strong column of his throat.

He jerked back, swallowed.

"Sky…"

She heard the warning in his voice—and the wanting.

And she saw both in the depths of those whiskey-colored eyes as they met and held her own.

"Jake," she answered softly.

A muscle in his jaw flexed, but he gave her no indication of anything he was thinking or feeling. No hint of anything at all before he said, "I knew you were going to be trouble the first minute I saw you."

But even those words were hardly more than a whisper from his lips before they captured hers.

Chapter Four

She'd fantasized about kissing Jake.

Maybe not by the side of the highway, but the setting didn't matter.

It only mattered that he was kissing her.

True, she didn't know much about him, but there was something between them. It had been there from the beginning, an unexpected spark that quickly ignited a flame. From the beginning, she'd wanted him. And now that the mystery of Molly's identity had been solved, there was no reason to deny what she wanted. What they both wanted.

Because the way Jake was kissing her, she no longer had any doubt that he wanted her, too.

So what if he wasn't a great conversationalist?

He *was* a great kisser.

His tongue swept along the seam of her lips, then slipped inside when she opened for him. Willingly. Eagerly. She pressed herself against him, welcoming the deeper intimacy. Wanting more.

As his mouth moved over hers, hot flames of desire spread through her veins, heating her body, melting her bones. She lifted her hands to his shoulders, needing something solid and steady to hold on to as the earth tilted beneath her feet and the world spun around her.

There were probably a dozen reasons that this was a bad idea. Not the least of which was that she hardly knew anything about him. It had taken weeks for Jake to even tell her his name, but despite his reticence, he wasn't self-absorbed. While their subsequent conversations had been brief, they'd nevertheless given her glimpses of his intelligence and humor. And though he'd only once mentioned a niece, he'd spoken of the child with affection.

Maybe the details that she knew about him were slim, but they were enough for Sky—especially in combination with the powerful chemistry between them. And she decided that kissing Jake couldn't possibly be a bad idea when it felt so incredibly good.

He slid his hands beneath the hem of her sweater, then over the bare skin of her abdomen, making her shiver. His palms were wide and callused, but his touch was gentle, raising goose bumps on her flesh.

It had been a long time since she'd had a man's hands on her, and she gloried in the feel of Jake's touch now. When his thumbs brushed the undersides of her breasts through the whisper-thin satin of her bra, she felt her nipples draw into tight points, begging to be noticed, touched, tasted. And she knew that she wouldn't have protested if he'd lowered his mouth to her breast right there at the side of the road.

Instead, he pulled his hands out from under her top and eased his lips from hers. "Car."

"What?" she said, resisting the urge to whimper in protest of his withdrawal.

"Car," he said again, as a vehicle came around the bend.

Sky recognized the white truck and its driver before he pulled up alongside her Jeep.

"Engine trouble?" Oscar Weston guessed. "Anything I can give you a hand with?"

She smiled to show her appreciation for the mechanic's offer, even as she shook her head. "Already fixed."

A furrow appeared between Oscar's bushy white brows as his gaze slid from Sky to Jake, before shifting back again. "Are you sure there's nothing I can do?"

"I'm sure," Sky said. "It's all good. But thanks."

The man gave a slow nod, sent Jake another hard look, then continued on his way.

"Sorry about that—about Mr. Weston, I mean," she hastened to clarify. "Not about the kiss."

"You don't have to apologize," he said. "But maybe I should."

"Don't you dare," she said.

He seemed taken aback by her vehement response—and maybe just a little bit amused.

"Okay, I won't," he agreed.

She nodded. "Good."

"So are we just going to forget it ever happened?"

Now she shook her head. "I don't want to forget it happened."

Jake's eyes held hers for a long moment before he asked, "What do you want, Sky?"

She replied without hesitation. "You."

His pupils flared even as he took a deliberate step back. "You don't know anything about me."

It wasn't just a statement but a warning, and one that she should probably heed. But for some inexplicable reason, everything she didn't know about Jake didn't matter as much as what she did—that she felt safe in his arms. Desirable. Desired.

For the past few years, she'd tried so hard to be the person everyone else needed that she'd neglected her own needs. Those needs were letting themselves be heard now, loud and clear.

"I know enough," she told him. And then she smiled. "Including where you live."

He swallowed. "Be sure, Sky."

She answered without hesitation. "I am."

He gave a short nod. "I'll follow you—just in case you have any more car trouble."

Sky was trembling still as she slid behind the wheel of her car and turned her key in the ignition, mentally crossing her fingers that her fuel injectors weren't damaged and her car would start. Because now that she'd decided what was going to happen next, she was eager to get there.

The engine coughed and sputtered…then turned over and fired.

Exhaling a grateful sigh, she shifted into drive and headed toward the sprawling log bungalow she'd always known as the Ferguson place.

Ross Ferguson had struggled as a cattle rancher, not because he was unwilling to do the work but because his heart wasn't in it. He'd eventually turned his attention and talent to making furniture from reclaimed wood, creating beautiful pieces and quickly gaining a reputation for himself within the local community.

Unfortunately, there wasn't a lot of demand for his work or a lot of money to be made, and his wife's ongoing battle with Cystic fibrosis meant that there were always medical bills to be paid. So Ross decided to supplement his income by leasing most of his land to the Circle G—an arrangement that was, as far as Sky knew, ongoing to this day.

But she wasn't thinking about Ross Ferguson's legal arrangement with her father as she pulled into the driveway. And at another time she might have stopped to admire the flowers blooming in the beds around the perimeter of the house, perennials that had been planted by Anna Ferguson years earlier. Right now, though, she was more interested in seeing the inside of the house—especially Jake's bedroom.

She stepped out of her Jeep, her heart pounding

with excitement and anticipation, as Jake pulled his truck into the double driveway beside her SUV.

As soon as he opened the door, Molly scrambled out, racing over to greet Sky.

"Yes, hello again," she said, crouching to fuss over the dog. "I came for a visit, if that's all right with you."

"Molly loves when people come to visit. She barks at anyone outside the door, but a guard dog she is not. As soon as they cross the threshold, she's all about making friends."

"Are we going to be friends?" Sky asked the dog.

Molly promptly rolled onto her back, splaying her legs to expose her belly for a rub.

"I'll take that as a yes," she said, indulging the animal's wordless request.

Jake slid a key into the lock of the side door, then held it open for Sky to enter.

A kaleidoscope of butterflies danced and twirled in her belly as she stepped over the threshold and into what was obviously the kitchen. According to her brother-in-law, Jake had been living in Haven for a few months now, but looking around the room, Sky was pretty confident that he hadn't been busy decorating during that time.

The white Shaker cabinets were simple and classic, but the green plastic knobs on the cupboard doors and the faux marble laminate countertop screamed of a bygone era. Several of the green and white checkerboard floor tiles were chipped or cracked and the

Formica table and chairs looked as if they belonged in a fifties diner.

She perched on the edge of one of those chairs to take off her boots, setting them on the mat beside the door. Jake unlaced his—combat rather than cowboy, she noted—and toed them off.

He tucked his hands in the front pockets of his jeans and rocked back on his heels. "Can I get you anything?" he offered. "Are you hungry? Thirsty?"

"I didn't come here for food or drink," she said, moving past him and into what was obviously the living room. The furniture was more modern in here, she noted, the oversize leather pieces and enormous flat screen a stark contrast to the faded floral paper on the walls.

"I know," Jake admitted, following behind her. "But I'm trying to give you a chance to come to your senses."

"I'll be sensible tomorrow," she said. "Right now, I really want you to kiss me again."

"And I really want to kiss you," he said, already dipping his head.

She sighed, a sound of pure pleasure, as his mouth captured hers. He kissed her deeply, hungrily, seducing her with the brush of his lips, the sweep of his tongue. It wasn't just a kiss, it was a promise of so much more, and the realization had excitement coursing through her veins, making her knees weak and her thighs quiver.

Because right here, right now, this was what she wanted.

He was what she wanted.

"Take me to bed, Jake."

He responded by scooping her into his arms, making Sky's already-fluttering heart beat faster inside her chest.

Molly, perhaps suspecting that they were playing a game, streaked past them and into the bedroom, leaping onto the bed.

He paused in the doorway and winced. "I, uh, wasn't planning on inviting anyone to come home with me," he said, setting Sky on her feet.

"I invited myself," she reminded him, giving the room a quick perusal.

It was simply and sparsely furnished, with a queen-size bed flanked by matching night tables on one wall and a long chest of drawers opposite.

"Still, if I'd thought there was anything greater than a snowball's chance in hell that I'd bring female company home, I would have put clean sheets on the bed," Jake told her. "And moved that pile of clothes on the chair to the laundry room. And checked the expiration date on the condoms in my toiletry bag."

"I've got some in my purse—condoms, not clean sheets," she clarified.

"Good to know," he said, reaching for the edge of the comforter.

The lump beneath the sheet wiggled.

He pulled it back and pointed to the door. "Out."

Molly lifted her paws to cover her face.

Sky couldn't help it—she giggled.

Jake slanted her a look. "Don't encourage her."

"I'm sorry," she said, not really sorry at all. "She's just too adorable."

"Yeah, she's adorable," he agreed. "But right now, she's also in the way." He turned back to the playful canine. "Molly?"

She dropped one paw, peeking at him with one eye.

"It's not playtime," he said firmly.

The dog let the other paw fall away and tilted her head to look at him imploringly.

"Out," he said, and pointed to the door again.

Molly inched toward the edge of the mattress, moving as slowly as possible, as if to give him a chance to change his mind.

Sky pressed her lips together to hold back another laugh as Jake grabbed the dog's collar and tugged her toward the door, closing it firmly when Molly was on the other side.

Then he looked back at the tangle of sheets again and said, "Do you want to wait in the living room for a few minutes while I sort things out in here?"

"No," Sky said, but tempered her refusal with a smile.

"No?" he echoed.

"There's no point in making the bed now when we're just going to mess it up again."

From the other side of the door came a plaintive whine.

"I have to admit, I feel a little guilty that she's been kicked out of her own room," Sky said, having spotted the dog bed in the corner.

"Molly thinks every room in the house is hers," he said. "In five minutes, she'll be settled on her favorite chair in the living room and forget that she was ever banished from here."

"And what will we be doing in five minutes?" Sky asked, lifting her sweater over her head and carelessly dropping it on the floor.

"Not talking about the dog," he promised, watching as she unzipped her skirt and wiggled it over her hips, leaving her standing before him in only a hot pink satin bra and turquoise lace panties. His eyes were dark as they skimmed over her slowly, approvingly. "I should have guessed you weren't a white cotton kind of girl."

"I like color," she said. "Though I would have matched my underwear if I'd known they were going to be on display."

"I like what you're wearing," he assured her. "But I think I'm going to like you wearing nothing at all even more."

He kissed her deeply then, wrapping his arms around her and pulling her close so their bodies were aligned, breasts to chest, thigh to thigh and all the interesting points in between.

But still it wasn't enough. She wanted skin on skin contact. And he was wearing far too many clothes.

She tugged the hem of his shirt out of his jeans and slid her hands beneath the fabric, exploring the smooth, taut muscles of his abdomen and chest with eager hands. He broke the kiss long enough to pull down the shade over the window, then yank the shirt over his head and toss it aside.

She caught a glimpse of a tattoo on his shoulder—the logo and motto of the USMC in glorious color confirming her suspicion that Jake had served in the military. There was more ink on his other arm, something that almost looked like a list, but it was hard to decipher in the dim light and, truthfully, she was more interested in his muscles than his body art at present. And the man did have spectacular muscles.

Her fingertips skimmed over sculpted abs as they traveled south to unfasten his belt. He helped her there, too, quickly shucking his jeans to reveal a pair of sexy black knit boxers—and an impressive erection. They tumbled together on top of the unmade bed, mouths mating, hands searching, each of them desperate to feel and touch and taste.

She'd only met him a few weeks earlier, so how was it that she felt as if she'd been waiting for him forever? Wanted him forever? As if he might finally be the one to—

No.

She firmly shoved that romanticized notion out of her mind. She'd spent far too much time during her teen years trying to fill the emptiness inside her with the attention of boys she wanted to believe actually cared about her. Most of them only cared about scoring—and lied if they didn't.

It was a long time after she'd graduated from high school before she realized that she was responsible for her own happiness, and it took her a few more years after that to find it. But she was happy now. Sure, she had unfulfilled hopes and dreams and three part-time jobs instead of a defined career path, but she was confident that her life was on track to get her where she wanted to go.

Jake wasn't part of her long-term plan, and being here with him now wasn't about anything more than finishing what they'd started with a single earth-tilting kiss on the side of the highway. Because in addition to taking responsibility for herself, Sky had also learned that she didn't need to be ashamed of wanting sex for the sake of sex.

Maybe she wasn't proud of her sometimes less-than-discriminating choices when she was younger, but she was a woman now, with a woman's needs. And it had been far too long since those needs had been satisfied.

But Jake was already on his way to changing that. With every brush of his lips, he communicated his desire. With every stroke of his hands, he stoked the fire that burned inside her. He rained kisses along her jaw, down her throat, then lower still. He nuzzled the hollow between her breasts, his shadowed jaw rasping against her tender skin. Then he found the center clasp of her bra and deftly unfastened it, peeling back the cups to bare her breasts to his avid gaze and eager mouth.

His lips skimmed over the tight bud of one nipple, a fleeting, teasing caress. She bit down on her bottom lip to keep from whimpering, pleading—*More.*

Please.—as his mouth shifted to her other breast, another teasing caress.

Deciding that turnabout was fair play, she let her hand brush over the front of his shorts and heard him suck in a breath. She stroked the hard length of him through the soft cotton with a fingertip, up and then down again, the deliberate action eliciting a low groan from deep in his throat. But the teasing caresses weren't enough for either of them, and she started to dip her fingers beneath the waistband of his briefs.

Jake caught her wrist and gently pulled her hand away.

"Give me a sec," he said, before rolling off the bed and disappearing into the adjoining bathroom.

He returned with a square packet in his hand. "I checked the date," he said, as he set the condom on the bedside table.

"We're good?"

One corner of his mouth kicked up in a half smile. "I'm hoping."

Sky smiled, too, as she drew him back down onto the mattress with her. "Well, let's find out," she suggested.

His hands moved boldly over her body, callused palms stroking her skin, sending tingles through her body.

Though he'd drawn the shade, so that only a thin ribbon of light from the late afternoon sun was allowed to squeeze through on either side, she could feel areas of puckered skin beneath her fingertips.

At first, she'd assumed he wanted the shade closed because the window was at ground level, despite the fact that the house was set back from the road and there were unlikely to be any passers-by this far on the outskirts of town. But now she wondered if he'd shut out the light so that she wouldn't see his scars.

Yeah, this wounded warrior definitely had a story to tell. And while Sky couldn't deny a certain curiosity about his military experience, she was more interested in the man himself, and she set about exploring his taut, hard body with her hands and her lips.

He captured her mouth again, his kiss hot and hungry, impatient and demanding, reflecting the same desperate urgency that was building inside her. There was no sweet seduction between them, only heat and passion and need.

"Now, Jake. Please."

He didn't make her ask twice, and she gasped as he thrust inside of her. Her orgasm came hard and fast, crashing over her in wave after wave of pleasure, leaving her stunned and breathless and with a vague thought that the celibacy vow she'd taken almost three years earlier had blown up in spectacular fashion.

Then he began to move inside her, and before she had a chance to draw air into her lungs, the tension started to build again. The glorious friction created by his rhythmic thrusts was almost more than she could bear. And though she wouldn't have thought it was possible to come again while her body was still quivering with the aftershocks of her first orgasm, she was overjoyed to be proven wrong.

The wind roared in his ears. Tiny grains of sand, whipped into a frenzy, slashed like knives. In the distance, a billowing cloud of dust. Harmless enough in the moment, it would be upon them quickly, reducing visibility to zero, blocking out even the sun.

Jake felt a hand on his arm. Soft. Gentle.

An unmistakably feminine touch.

No, it wasn't the wind he heard, but the blood pulsing through his veins.

He jolted back to the present and exhaled a long, slow breath as his heart continued to pound like a jackhammer inside his chest.

"Yeah," he decided. "We're good."

Sky chuckled softly. "You're not going to get any argument from me."

Though his body wasn't just sated but spent, he managed to lift his weight off her and roll onto his back.

He hadn't realized how much he'd missed sex until his body was joined together with hers. It was more than just the physical act of mating or the culmination of mutual desire. It was the sense of connection, of becoming a part of something bigger than himself. A connection that he'd been certain he'd lost forever when—

No. He wasn't going to go back there now.

He was just going to let himself be in this moment for the moment.

So resolved, he closed his eyes, a surprising feeling of peace stealing over his body, relaxing his muscles. He actually started to drift off, thinking it might be nice to fall asleep with a warm woman in his arms—and wake with her beside him.

Yeah, it might be nice.

Or it might be a nightmare.

With that sobering thought at the front of his mind, he rolled out of bed and headed to the bathroom to get rid of the condom and get his head on straight—not an easy task when he was feeling so unaccustomedly satisfied and relaxed.

He hadn't planned for this. He wouldn't have dared to even dream it might happen. And just because it had happened—and had been pretty amazing—he knew it would be a mistake to think that the pleasure he'd shared with Sky could ever lead to anything more.

He'd come to Haven because he needed some time and distance to get his life back on track. The absolute last thing he needed was the complication of a woman.

But he couldn't deny that he'd enjoyed being with her.

She was spontaneous and passionate and fun, and while their bodies were intimately linked, she'd made him feel as if he was not just alive but whole and normal.

Unfortunately, he knew that was only an illusion.

But as he recalled the way she'd touched him, her hands stroking every inch of his body, he knew there was no way she'd missed his scars. But she hadn't skipped a beat when she'd encountered the ridges of puckered skin that were an unwanted souvenir of his last tour. Her touch might have gentled as she'd traced the rough edges, but she hadn't recoiled. She hadn't turned away.

And she hadn't asked any questions.

If he was a man capable of opening his heart, he might love her for that alone.

But he wasn't.

Still, he stood there for a moment, looking at her in his bed. The sheet was pulled up high enough to cover the swell of her exquisite breasts, but one of her legs—slim and toned and perfect—was thrown over the top, and her silky dark hair was fanned out over his pillow. She looked so peaceful and contented, as if there was nowhere else she wanted to be, and he felt a tug of something that might have been regret that he had to disturb her.

"Skylar?"

Her eyelids flickered before they lifted, revealing blue-gray eyes that he longed to get lost in. Then her lips curved, and his body—though recently sated—stirred again.

"Mmm?" she murmured.

It was as much an invitation as an acknowledgment—an invitation that he desperately wished he could accept. He wanted to slip between the sheets with her again, spread her legs wide and—

He ruthlessly stomped down on his growing desire and said, "You have to go."

Chapter Five

Well, that was a new experience, Sky acknowledged, sitting behind the wheel of her Jeep and staring at the closed door of Jake Kelly's house.

Not the sex—although that had exceeded her expectations in the very best way—but what had followed. His summary dismissal of her had been not just surprising but insulting.

Okay, so maybe he liked his own space when he slept. He wouldn't be the first guy who had no interest in cuddling a woman after the deed was done. But instead of rolling over and falling asleep, like a few other guys she'd known, he'd told her to leave.

Bluntly and unapologetically.

And staring at the door he'd closed between them, she couldn't help but feel as if she'd been used.

Which she knew wasn't really fair, because if any using had been done, it had been mutual—and mutually satisfying. And while the logical part of her brain understood that there might be something more going on here, that possibility did nothing to soothe the unexpected ache in the region of her heart.

You don't know anything about me.

Yeah, she definitely should have heeded his warning.

Because while she had no doubts that he'd enjoyed the physical act, it was more than apparent to Sky that Jake didn't want anything more.

Of course, if he'd given her the benefit of even five minutes of conversation, she might have been able to reassure him that she wasn't looking for any kind of a relationship right now, either. And that even if she was, she wouldn't set her sights on a moody Marine with obvious intimacy issues.

No matter that they'd had mind-numbing, heart-pounding, body-tingling sex together.

And no matter how much she wanted to experience it again.

She had too much pride and self-respect to chase after any man—especially one who had clearly and unequivocally given her the brush-off.

Of course, she had only herself to blame. He'd told her, the first night he'd sat at Diggers' bar, that he wasn't interested in company or conversation. Obviously he was a man who said what he meant and meant what he said, and she was an idiot for not paying closer attention. Or maybe she was a fool for allowing herself to believe that things had changed over the past few weeks.

Either way, the current situation was no one's fault but her own.

She backed out of the driveway, but she couldn't resist turning her head for one last glance toward Jake's house and saw Molly at the window. Well, at least the dog seemed disappointed to watch her go.

He'd totally blown that.

As Jake stood in the kitchen, staring at the door through which Sky had recently exited, he acknowledged that there were countless other things he could have said or done to communicate his desire for her to leave without resorting to the blunt words he'd used. But when he'd returned to his bedroom after discarding the condom and saw her temptingly naked body sprawled on top of the tangled sheets, he hadn't wanted her to leave at all. What he'd wanted then was to get back into bed with her for an encore performance—Hot, Sweaty Sex, Part Two.

But he was afraid that if he gave in to that desire, he wouldn't want to let her go.

And the one thing he knew for certain was that he couldn't let her stay.

Molly turned away from the living room window and padded into the kitchen. She sat at his feet, looking up at him with big brown eyes filled with sadness.

"I know," he said, acknowledging the truth aloud. "I blew it."

She tilted her head, as if to let him know that she was listening, although her understanding seemed to be limited to the words *walk, run, ride, fetch* and *dinner.*

"Of course, I blew it," he continued. "I'm not ready for a relationship. I barely know how to have a conversation with regular people anymore, never mind interact on a deeper level."

Except that he'd had no difficulty interacting with Sky in his bedroom, and on a very deep level. But he knew he shouldn't feel too proud about that, because the way she'd kept her gaze averted as she gathered up her clothes and dressed, he didn't think he was likely to ever see her naked again.

"It's pretty sad, isn't it, when the most meaningful conversations I have are with my dog?"

Molly tilted her head so far over, he was afraid she was going to end up with a kink in her neck.

"Especially when you're just hanging out with me because you want your dinner," he noted.

Recognizing the word *dinner,* Molly immediately sprang to her feet and danced over to her bowl.

Jake measured out her kibble and dumped it into the bowl.

Then he turned on the oven to heat up a frozen pizza for himself, wishing—for the first time in a long time—that he had someone to share it with.

When Sky got back to the Circle G, she found Ashley at the kitchen table, gluing letters onto a poster board.

It had taken some time for Sky and her siblings to accept that they had a half sister, and longer still for them to acknowledge that their father had real feelings for his youngest daughter's mom. Not just because he'd grieved the death of his first wife so deeply and for so long, but because Valerie was a Blake and the Gilmore-Blake feud was the stuff of legends in Haven, Nevada, with tangled roots that went back five generations.

Now David Gilmore and Valerie Blake were married and Ashley was sleeping in the bedroom across the hall from Sky. And while it had been a surprise to Sky to discover that she had a little sister, she was enjoying getting to know Ashley.

"Homework on a Saturday night?" Sky asked her now.

Ashley nodded. "It's for book fair, and it's worth thirty percent of my final grade."

"How's it going?"

The teen made a face. "Me and Chloe are supposed to be working on it together, but she left."

Sky opened the fridge, took out a can of cola. "Do you need a caffeine boost?"

"Sure, thanks."

She grabbed a second can and carried both to the table.

Ashley popped the tab on her drink, and a furry head popped up from her lap.

"You're not supposed to have the dog at the table," Sky felt compelled to remind her.

"But there's no food at the table," Ashley said, a

point that seemed to remind her: "Although Martina made a plate for you—it's in the oven."

"I guess I missed dinner, didn't I?"

And lunch, she remembered now, thinking of the forgotten takeout container on the backseat of her Jeep. But she wasn't hungry—or she didn't think she was, until her empty stomach rumbled.

"A plate of what?" she asked, even as she opened the oven door to take a peek.

"Meatless meatloaf, mashed potatoes and green beans."

"What did Dad have for dinner?" she wondered aloud, sliding her hand into an oven mitt to remove the hot plate.

Since David Gilmore's heart attack, Martina had been strict about limiting his intake of fatty foods, including red meat—which was a definite bone of contention between the cattle rancher and his long-time cook. And since Ashley and her mom had taken up residence at the Circle G, Martina had embraced the challenge of making occasional meatless meals to accommodate Ashley's vegetarian lifestyle.

"Meatless meatloaf, mashed potatoes and green beans," Ashley said again. "But Martina made his potatoes with skim milk instead of cream and didn't let him have any butter or salt on his beans."

She carried her plate and cutlery to the table. "Did he threaten to fire her?"

Ashley grinned. "Just like he does every day."

Sky picked up her fork and dug into the meatloaf and her sister got back to gluing the cardboard letters that would spell out her project title. But when Sky paused between bites, she noticed Ashley staring at her phone.

"Is everything okay?" she asked.

"What? Oh, yeah." Ashley capped the glue stick and picked up her can of soda, then set it down again without taking a sip. "Actually, I was just thinking about Jodie."

Sky paused with a forkful of mashed potatoes halfway to her mouth. "Who?"

Ashley rolled her eyes. "I know you're not supposed to talk about your clients or patients or whatever they're called, but Chloe told me that her sister's been talking to you about their mom's boyfriend."

"Did she?" Sky said.

Though Jodie had mentioned that she had a sister, she hadn't realized that Jodie's sister was Ashley's best friend because the two girls had different last names.

"He doesn't pay any attention to my sister," Jodie had told Sky, when she'd first reported the uneasiness she felt around her mother's boyfriend.

But Sky knew that opportunity was often a deciding factor in the commission of sexual crimes.

And when she'd met with Jodie that afternoon and asked about her sister's whereabouts, Jodie had assured her that she was safe because she was spending the night at a friend's house. That revelation had alleviated Sky's immediate concerns, because she'd believed that the teen's mother would be home before Jodie's sister returned from her sleepover the following day.

Ashley nodded. "Chloe said Jodie freaked out when their mom told them that Leon would be moving in with them, but she also said that Jodie can be a drama queen at times."

Sky pushed aside her half-eaten plate of food. "What does Chloe think about her mom's boyfriend?"

"She says he's not so bad. He even pretends not to notice when she sneaks one of mom's vodka coolers out of the fridge."

Sky wasn't shocked to learn that her fourteen-year-old sister's best friend was sneaking alcohol, but she was increasingly uneasy with the picture coming together in her mind.

"You said Chloe was here earlier, working on this project with you?"

Ashley nodded.

"Was she supposed to sleep over?"

"Yeah, but then she decided that she'd rather go see a movie."

"Who was she going to the movie with?"

Ashley shrugged. "She didn't say, just that Leon was going to pick her up and we'd finish the poster board another time."

Leon had picked her up?

Oh, this was so *not* good.

"You know, it isn't really fair that you're spending your Saturday night working on this project while

Chloe is out having fun," Sky said, aiming for a casual tone.

"I know," Ashley agreed. "But what can I do?"

"You can call Chloe right now and tell her that we're on our way to pick her up so that she can come back here and help finish the project, like she promised."

Sky slept through breakfast the next morning, and after a quick shower, she decided to go into town to grab a bite. On the way there, she decided that she needed some sisterly advice as much as she needed sustenance, so she stopped at Sweet Caroline's before heading over to Katelyn and Reid's house.

"I brought coffee—and donuts," Sky said, holding up the tray of drinks and bag of pastries.

"She looks like my sister, but she's really the devil," Kate remarked, accepting the proffered items.

"You don't have to eat any, if you don't want to," she pointed out.

"The problem is that I want to eat them all."

"Well, at least save one of the jelly-filled for Tessa," Sky suggested, as her niece came running down the hall.

"Auntie 'ky! Auntie 'ky!" The little girl launched herself at her aunt. Sky caught her easily and lifted her for a smacking—and sticky—kiss.

"I think someone already had breakfast," she noted. "I taste maple syrup."

"An' pancakes," Tessa said, already wiggling to be

let down. Since she'd taken her first steps, it seemed to Sky that the little girl never stayed still.

Sure enough, as soon as she set her niece back on the ground, Tessa took off, eager to play.

Ah, the life of a two-and-a-half-year-old, Sky thought, with amusement and affection, as she followed her sister to the dining room.

"Reid took her to the Morning Glory Café so that I could sleep in a little," Kate told her.

"Are you not feeling well?" Sky's tone was deliberately casual as she pried the lid from her cup.

"Just tired," Kate said. "Which isn't as much of a surprise this time around, but still a struggle."

"This time?" Sky grinned. "So he was right? You *are* pregnant?"

Her sister nodded. "But it's still early days, so we're trying to keep the news quiet for a while yet."

She mimed zipping her lips.

"You know the not-so-quiet news making the rounds this morning?" Kate continued. "Leon Franks was arrested last night and charged with supplying alcohol to a minor."

Thanks to her stop at Sweet Caroline's, Sky had already heard the news. "Unfortunately, I don't imagine that will keep him locked up for long." In fact, she wouldn't be surprised to hear that the man had already made bail. But she was keeping her fingers crossed that, whether or not the charges stuck, Leon's arrest would be a wake-up call to Tammy Morningstar to get the man out of her house and out of her life. In the meantime, Sky had at least succeeded in getting an inebriated Chloe out of a potentially dangerous situation the night before—and helped Ashley glue together the pieces of her book fair project.

"Probably not," Kate acknowledged. "But the outstanding warrant from St. Paul, Minnesota on charges of possession of child pornography will."

That was news to Sky, and she immediately knew that she had her brother-in-law to thank for following up her request. "I'm not glad that Jodie's instincts were right about this guy, but I'm relieved that he's going to be Minnesota's problem. I assume he'll be extradited to face those charges?"

Kate nodded. "The DA's filling out the paperwork this morning."

"That's a relief," Sky decided.

"Now tell me your news," her sister suggested.

"I don't have any news."

"Are you sure?" Kate pressed. "Because the coffee and donuts suggest otherwise."

"Maybe I did want some advice," she admitted.

"About?"

"Men."

"As a species in general? Or are you referring to someone specific?" Kate asked.

"Jake Kelly."

"Oh?"

Something in her sister's deliberately casual tone tripped her radar. "Do you know him?"

Kate's gaze slid away. "Not really."

"He's a client," she guessed.

"No, but... I guess it's not really a violation of

attorney-client privilege to tell you that Ross Ferguson was. And it's hardly a secret that Jake is the nephew that Ross named as primary beneficiary in his will." Kate looked at her sister then. "But how do you know him?"

"He's been in the bar a few times." Actually, Jake had come into Diggers' six times while Sky was working, but she didn't want her sister to know that she'd been counting.

"And he's a lousy tipper?" Kate guessed.

She managed a smile. "No, he's a decent tipper. But he's a lousy conversationalist."

"So maybe not everyone who sits at the bar is looking for a tête-à-tête with the bartender," her sister suggested.

"But most customers are at least willing to exchange basic pleasantries," Sky said. "It was weeks before Jake even told me his name."

"A man's entitled to his privacy," Kate pointed out.

"I know," she agreed. "But there's something about him—"

"No," her sister interjected firmly.

Sky frowned. "No what?"

"You have enough wounded souls in your life without looking to add another one."

"What makes you think he's a wounded soul?"

Kate pressed her lips together, apparently already having said more than she'd intended to.

"You know that he's former military," Sky guessed.

"That's the rumor around town," her sister conceded.

"And this time, the rumor is actually true. Jake was—or *is*—a Marine."

"Did he tell you that?" Kate asked.

Sky shook her head. "He didn't have to. I saw his US Marine Corps tattoo."

"I've never noticed a tattoo."

"It's on his shoulder, so you wouldn't notice it if he's wearing a shirt."

Her sister's brows winged up. "Are you telling me that you saw him without a shirt on?"

"I saw him with nothing on," Sky confided.

"Oh. My. God." Kate's jaw dropped. "You *slept* with him?"

Her smile slipped, as her sister's question pointedly reminded her that there'd been no sleeping because Jake had kicked her out of his bed as soon as the deed was done. "No, but I did have sex with him."

"But you just told me that you don't know anything about this guy," Kate said, sounding worried.

"How well did you know Reid before you fell into bed with him?" Sky countered.

Her sister's cheeks colored. "Not as well as I should have, or I might have been prepared for him to show up in town a few weeks later wearing the sheriff's badge."

"Then you have no right to judge me," she pointed out.

"I'm not judging, I'm worried."

"Don't be," Sky said. "I know how to look out for myself."

"You were careful?" her sister prompted.

"Always," she promised.

"So was I," Kate reminded her. "Which was all well and good until a condom broke."

She was referring, of course, to the first night she'd spent with her now-husband, Reid Davidson, at a legal conference in Carson City.

"And nine months later, you had a beautiful baby girl," Sky noted.

Kate smiled then. "But that doesn't mean I've forgotten those terrifying moments in the beginning when I was completely overwhelmed and didn't have the first clue what to do."

Sky hadn't forgotten, either—or the guilt she'd felt when her sister told her about the broken condom. Sky had been the one to give Kate the box before her sister went away, to ensure she'd be protected if the opportunity presented itself. Thankfully, everything had worked out for Katelyn and Reid—and Tessa—in the end.

"Well, you don't have to worry," Sky assured her sister now. "There weren't any safety malfunctions when I was with Jake."

"That's good then," Kate said, though she still sounded dubious. "Do you think…are you going to… see him again?"

Sky shrugged, a deliberately casual gesture. "I'm sure our paths will cross."

But the truth was, Sky wasn't sure about anything where Jake Kelly was concerned.

Chapter Six

In the Marine Corps, Jake had learned the importance of being prepared for any contingency—and that, despite those preparations, it was almost inevitable that things would go FUBAR.

Since moving to Haven, he was trying to embrace routines as a way of feeling more in control of his life. According to the doctor he'd talked to at the VA hospital, routine was supposed to help him cope with change, form healthy habits and reduce his stress levels. Over the past couple of months, part of his routine had been Wednesday night meetings with a veterans' support group at the community center, followed by what he dubbed "immersion therapy" at Diggers'.

Though he had yet to share anything of his own

experiences with the group, he did find some comfort in listening to and empathizing with the experiences of others, proof that he wasn't alone in his struggles to readjust to civilian life. But since that first night when he decided to stop at Diggers' on his way home, his routine had evolved to include a pint of beer at the local bar and grill—and occasionally some casual flirting with the pretty bartender.

Except that now he'd done a lot more than flirt with Sky Gilmore, he found himself in a bit of a dilemma. Should he stick with his usual routine, come directly home after the meeting or opt to stay in for the evening altogether?

He glanced over at his dog, who was stretched out in the sun by the open doors of the converted barn while Jake tidied up what had been his uncle's workspace. When he'd first arrived in Haven and walked into the house where he'd spent a couple of weeks every summer with his aunt and uncle, he'd been assailed by the memories. He could almost see Fred and George—red-haired Irish setters named for the Weasley twins from Harry Potter—jumping and playing in the yard, and could almost smell the scent of cinnamon lingering in the air, as if there was a tray of Aunt Anna's snickerdoodle cookies ready to come out of the oven. But what he remembered most was the love and the laughter, so much so that it seemed to echo in every room.

Yes, Ross had struggled to make a go of it as a rancher, and Anna had battled with health difficulties, but no one who'd spent any time with them would doubt how much they'd loved one another. Though Jake had been taken aback to learn that his uncle had passed within six months of his wife, he realized he shouldn't have been surprised. Ross had often said that Anna was his heart, and without her, there was nothing left to pump life through his veins.

It had been difficult enough for Jake to walk through the front door of their house and know that he wouldn't ever see either of them again. It was even more difficult for him to enter the workshop, where he'd spent so many hours with his uncle during the annual summer visits that were intended to give his parents some time alone together. Even as a kid, Jake had known that he would be a Marine one day, and Ross had never tried to steer him in a different direction. But his uncle had thought it was important for a boy to know how to use some basic tools, and his instructions had been careful, his patience endless and his forgiveness of Jake's mistakes sincere.

"You can't make an omelet without breaking a few eggs," he'd liked to say.

Jake had broken a lot of eggs.

There were bits and pieces of wood scattered around the workshop now, as if his uncle had been sorting through them to find what he wanted for his current project. But there were no plans pinned up on the pegboard, nothing to indicate what, if anything, he had been working on.

Jake's cell phone rang, distracting him from his task, and he set the wood chisel back down on the workbench before picking up the phone. He swiped the screen to connect the call. "Hey, Mom. What's up?"

"I was just thinking about you," Barbara Kelly replied.

When he'd first moved to Haven, she'd "thought about" him several times every day, until he'd threatened to stop answering her numerous calls. Now they talked once a week, on Sunday afternoons. That wasn't to say that she didn't reach out to him otherwise, but she always had a specific purpose for doing so.

"Any particular reason?" he prompted, wondering if he might have forgotten about a special occasion.

Courtesy of the brain injury that was an unwanted souvenir from Iraq, he'd forgotten a lot of things when he first came home. Most of his memories had eventually returned, along with his ability to assimilate and retain new information, but there were still pieces missing.

Was today one of those pieces?

Was it his mom's birthday?

No, that was in November.

"I thought you should know that Margot and Tim are getting married," she said.

The news didn't surprise him. More important, it didn't elicit any kind of emotional response, except relief that it wasn't something he should have known about. Aside from that, he truly didn't care.

"Why are you telling me?" he asked.

"Because I didn't want you to hear it from someone else," she admitted.

"Because you thought it would upset me," he guessed.

"Doesn't it?" she asked gently.

"No."

"You must feel something," she pressed. "It wasn't all that long ago that Margot was wearing your ring."

As if he needed to be reminded.

He'd put the ring on Margot's finger before he went to Iraq the first time, because she'd wanted some kind of tangible reassurance that he was committed to her, to help her through the lonely nights while he was away.

"Our engagement ended more than two years ago, Mom."

"But how do you feel?" she pressed.

Because his mom always wanted him to talk about his feelings, preferring to believe that he was keeping his emotions bottled up rather than that he wasn't capable of feeling anything anymore.

"I feel fine," he said.

Okay, fine was a stretch—or maybe even an outright lie—but as far as his former fiancée's wedding plans were concerned, he really couldn't care less.

"Well, that's good then, because you're going to get an invitation to the wedding."

"How do you know this?"

"Margot called and asked me for your address."

He didn't have to ask if she'd given it. It would never have occurred to his mom to refuse such a request. Instead, he only said, "You should have told her not to waste a stamp."

"You were friends for a long time. You and Margot and Tim," she reminded him gently.

"And then Margot and Tim got *really* friendly when I was in rehab."

"It was a difficult time for everyone."

"Yeah, but only one of us was recovering from a blast injury and enduring hours of daily therapy."

"You're still angry," she noted.

He sighed. "No, Mom. I'm not still angry. I'm just not prepared to celebrate a relationship built on a foundation of deceit and disloyalty."

"Going to the wedding would prove that you're over her."

"I don't have to prove anything to anyone, least of all the girl who screwed around with my former best friend."

"I'm not making excuses for what they did—"

"Good," Jake said, cutting her off.

Barbara's sigh was a reluctant acknowledgment that the topic was closed. "Okay then, tell me when you're going to come home."

"I don't know."

"We miss you," she said.

He knew what she really meant was that *she* missed him, and he missed her, too. But he knew it was best for everyone if he stayed away for a while.

Or maybe forever.

"Well, if you're not planning to come home anytime soon, maybe we could come to Haven to see you," she suggested.

"You'd be bored to death here," he said, offering her an out.

Because the truth was, while his mother might be content enough to revisit the town where she'd grown up and where her brother had remained throughout his adult life, Jake knew she'd never convince his father to come.

As far as Jake could recall, his father had visited Haven exactly once, and had grumbled the whole time that he was there. Major William Robert Kelly had never been a fan of his brother-in-law and he didn't pretend otherwise. In his opinion, Ross was either a quitter or a failure, because after struggling for a lot of years as a cattle rancher, he'd chosen to sell off his stock and lease his land rather than knuckling down and working harder.

"Knuckle down and work harder" was a big thing with the Major. He wasn't entirely unsympathetic to his youngest son, but he continued to espouse the belief that Jake should shake off his moods, get himself back into fighting shape and reenlist. He'd made no effort to hide his displeasure when Jake told him that he was moving to Haven for a while. Then again, he'd always seemed to resent that his youngest son enjoyed hanging out with his maternal uncle, even accusing his brother-in-law of filling Jake's head with sawdust dreams.

Maybe that was why Ross had put Jake's name on the title. According to the date on his will, it had been drafted after Jake had received his medical discharge from the Marine Corps. Maybe Ross understood that his nephew had failed, too, and this was his way of showing that there were always other opportunities in life. If only Jake had the courage to take them.

"I've gotta go, Mom," Jake said. "I've got a meeting tonight."

And then he'd see if he could get a cold beer without a colder shoulder from a certain sexy bartender.

When Wednesday rolled around again, Sky found herself alternately watching the clock—and cursing herself for doing so. Yet she couldn't resist another glance.

9:55 p.m.

And still no sign of Jake.

But why should she have expected anything different?

He certainly wasn't the first guy who'd dropped her like a hot potato as soon as she slept with him. And if she was disappointed, it was in herself as much as Jake, because she'd really thought she was making smarter choices now.

Next time, she promised herself.

"Next time what?" Mr. Virga asked her.

She smiled at the retired ophthalmologist. "Next time I'm talking to myself, I'll try to keep both sides of the conversation inside my head."

"They say that talking to—and even arguing with—yourself is okay," the old man said. "It's only when you lose those arguments that you should start to worry."

"Good to know," she said, and smiled as she rang up his bill and took his money.

When she turned back to give Mr. Virga his change, she saw Jake in his usual seat at the bar.

Her heart did a happy little dance inside her chest, but she kept her attention focused on her elderly customer.

"Thanks," she said, when he pushed a tip across the counter to her. "You have a good night now, Mr. Virga."

"I surely will," the old man said, with a wink.

Jake watched the exchange, his expression inscrutable.

"What are you having tonight?" she asked him, playing it cool.

"A pint of Sam Adams."

She grabbed a mug and held it under the tap. "One step forward, two steps back."

"I don't do well with change," he admitted.

"Is that why you're here? Because Wednesday night at Diggers' has become a habit?"

"Partly," he acknowledged.

She set the beer in front of him.

"But mostly because I wanted to see you—to explain."

"You don't owe me any explanations, Jake."

"I kind of feel like I do."

"Neither one of us made any promises. In fact, neither one of us said very much of anything," she remarked.

"I thought we communicated pretty well without words."

"I guess we did," she acknowledged.

His gaze slid to the side, as if to ensure no one was close enough to overhear their conversation. "But this is weird now, isn't it?"

"Does it feel weird?"

"A little," he said.

"Maybe that's because you kicked me out of your bed before I'd even managed to catch my breath after we had sex," she said, her tone deliberately light.

"About that... I'm sorry that I couldn't let you stay."

His remark only raised more questions in her mind, but since this wasn't the time or the place for that conversation, she only said, "Is Molly the jealous type?"

He smiled, apparently relieved that she wasn't pushing for more of an explanation. "More possessive than jealous, I'd say."

She dumped a scoop of ice into a highball glass, squeezed a wedge of lime, poured a shot of gin and added a splash of tonic from the soda gun. "Maybe she just needs to get to know me better," she suggested.

"I think that's a possibility worth exploring," he agreed, as he lifted the mug to his lips.

Sky poured the ingredients for a couple of Nevada cocktails into a shaker, gave it a vigorous shake, then strained the drink into martini glasses for Courtney to deliver. Catching her eye, Adrian Romanos lifted his empty glass. She nodded and tipped a mug beneath the tap to pour him another draft, then made her way down the bar to deliver it.

Adrian was a regular who spent a lot of hours—and more than a few dollars—at the bar, and Sky wasn't going to neglect him just because she'd rather be talking to—and maybe flirting with—Jake. Adrian also worked for the town planning department, and he was chatting with her about the proposed schedule of events for the upcoming Haven Heritage Day celebrations—including the addition of a charity softball game this year—when Jake finished his drink.

Though it would have been out of character for him to hang around after his glass was empty, she was still a little disappointed to watch him pull some money out of his wallet, tuck it under the bottom of his glass and walk out.

Proving to Sky that nothing had changed.

Sure, she'd had the most amazing sex of her life with the man, but he still didn't want her company or conversation.

Good thing she wasn't thin-skinned, or his disappearing act might have hurt her feelings.

Of course, it was her own fault for falling into bed with a man she knew nothing about. She could make excuses for her behavior—and it was true that she'd been feeling lonely and that it had been a very long time since she'd been intimate with a man. But it was also true that neither of those factors was as significant as the attraction she'd felt the first time Jake walked into the bar.

And while she was admittedly a little baffled by his actions, she suspected that Jake's determination to keep everyone at a distance was connected to the scars she'd discovered on his body. Or the invisible ones that he clearly carried inside.

You don't know anything about me.

But she wanted to.

The scars, along with military tattoo, suggested that he was a man who'd been through a lot. Though post-traumatic stress disorder wasn't her area of expertise, she was familiar with the basic origins and symptoms. Witnessing or experiencing a traumatic event could result in difficulties in social situations and personal relationships.

She imagined that many people who'd served in the military had witnessed or experienced traumatic events. And she wondered if Jake would ever open up to her enough to tell her about his experiences.

Of course, getting naked with the guy didn't give her any right to poke around in his head. And the fact that she'd been naked with him was a pretty solid reason for her *not* to be the one poking around in his head.

They'd had sex—they didn't have a relationship.

If she was under any illusions otherwise, his exit from the bar without so much as a goodbye had effectively obliterated them.

Sunday through Wednesday, Diggers' closed at midnight. Still, by the time the last lingering customers were gone, the receipts were tallied and the bar was tidied, it was almost 1:00 a.m. Sky exited through the kitchen, as she always did, waving to Marty—who was still up to his elbows in soapy water scrubbing pans—on her way out. The dishwasher usually walked to work, since he lived just down the street, so Sky was surprised to see a truck parked beside her SUV when she stepped outside.

Warning signs immediately flashed in her mind for a split second before recognition set in and she realized it was Jake's vehicle—and the man himself was leaning against the hood of the pickup.

Her heart, ignoring the warnings of her head, started to pound harder and faster.

She took a few steps closer. "What's the matter? Did you run out of gas?"

His lips twitched. "No."

She hadn't realized Molly was in the truck until the dog poked her head out of the open driver's side window.

Unable to resist the animal's imploring gaze, Sky lifted a hand and scratched the soft fur beneath her chin. "What are you doing out so late at night?"

"I told her what you said, about her needing to get to know you better, and she agreed it was a good idea," Jake said.

"And you thought *now* would be a good time for that?"

He shrugged. "I wanted to see you and I thought, even if you were mad at me, you wouldn't be able to resist her."

"I wasn't mad at you."

"You weren't happy with me."

"I'm not entirely sure what I feel," she admitted.

"That makes two of us," he confided.

He came closer, until they were nearly touching.

"I want you, Skylar." The words were barely more than a whisper in the night. "Even though I know I shouldn't, I can't seem to stop wanting you."

"Why do you think you shouldn't?"

"Because my life is seriously screwed up."

"Anything you want to talk about?" she asked him.

He shook his head.

"You just want to go back to your place and get naked together again?"

"It's not a very tempting offer, is it?" he acknowledged ruefully.

"It works for me," she said.

"Really?"

"Yeah. When you left the bar earlier tonight, I was convinced that the best sex of my life was going to be a one-night stand."

"The best sex of your life?" He grinned. "I'm flattered."

"Maybe *life* is an exaggeration," she said. "Prior to Saturday, it had been a really long time for me, so my perception might have been a little skewed."

"Or maybe you just need an encore performance to convince you."

Then he drew her into his arms and lowered his head to cover her lips with his own.

His hands slid up her back, a sensual caress,

then down again, over the curve of her buttocks. She could feel the evidence of his arousal pressed against her belly and thrilled in the knowledge that he was as turned on as she was.

The flood of desire through her veins was as familiar as the flavor of his kiss. She didn't know what it was about this man that made her respond to him so intensely, but she couldn't deny that she did.

And knew that she was in serious trouble.

Tonight, Jake's bed was made with clean sheets, his dirty clothes had been dumped in the hamper and he'd sprayed air freshener to get rid of any lingering doggy odors. He hoped Sky would be impressed, because Molly sure wasn't. His faithful companion had sneezed several times then tossed her head in the air and escaped to another part of the house. But she'd forgiven the indignity to her sensitive nose when he'd scooped up his keys and invited her to go for a ride.

Still, he found himself having second and third thoughts as he followed Sky's taillights through the dark night. Not about what *he* wanted—because he'd known what that was as soon as he'd walked into Diggers' tonight and saw her behind the bar—but about the mixed signals he was sending to her.

He'd tried to be honest about what he was and wasn't offering. And mutual pleasure was likely to be the extent of it. Truthfully, he hadn't been certain he'd be able to give her even that the first time. He'd known the parts were in working order, but he hadn't been intimate with a woman since long before he'd been sent home via medical transport—and even during the brief period after his return when he was still with Margot, neither his mind nor his body had been any condition for sex. But he didn't want to be thinking about that when he should be focused on seduction. And on Sky.

Though he had no doubt that he'd satisfied her the first time, they'd both been in a race to the finish. He was determined to show a little more patience this time—and a lot more finesse.

His determination lasted only until she touched him, the stroke of her soft hands on his hard body snapping the leash of his self-control. What was it about Sky Gilmore that made him want her with an intensity that bordered on desperation?

Was it the way her lips curved whenever she saw him walk into the bar, as if she'd been watching and waiting for him?

Was it the light in her eyes that seemed capable of illuminating the deepest darkness inside him?

Or was it simply the escapism that she offered?

Because when he was touching Sky, there was no room in his head for thoughts of anything else.

No worries. No remorse. No regrets.

There was only the sweet scent of her hair, the silky softness of her skin, the tantalizing seduction of her body.

She was slim and toned and, to his eyes, so absolutely perfect that he knew he—scarred as he was on the inside and out—could never be worthy of her. He wondered that she couldn't see it as clearly as he did, because if she did, whatever this was between them would already be over.

But he was selfish enough not to let that matter right now. He could ignore the fact that they were a real-life beauty and beast for the thrill of having her in his arms for a few more hours.

And he knew their time together was likely limited to that. He wasn't a man a woman made plans with for the future. If it had been true when he was on active duty, it was even more so now. There was so much she didn't know about him, and when she uncovered his secrets, it would change everything.

She'd shown admirable restraint so far, but she would inevitably want to know about his scars. And his tattoos. In fact, he was a little surprised she hadn't asked already. Surprised and grateful. Perhaps she sensed his reticence to talk about his past. Or maybe she was smart enough to have put the pieces together without the need to ask any questions—in which case she was undoubtedly smart enough to put some distance between them.

Right now, it was the intensity of the attraction between them that was getting in the way of her ability to see the situation clearly. And his, too.

But sex was one thing. Intimacy was something entirely different. And as much as he wished he could let her stay, he wasn't ready to fall asleep with her. Because it was in sleep that his guard was down and the dreams came. Dreams that he couldn't bear for her to witness. Not only because he didn't want her to know about the demons that plagued him, but because he worried that letting her stay might put her at risk.

Everyone knew stories about veterans who returned from assignment and lashed out at loved ones—parents or spouses or even children. Because in the midst of a flashback, a soldier, sailor, airman or Marine didn't see that parent or spouse or child, only a threat to be neutralized. Though he'd never woken up with a weapon in his hand, his training had made him a weapon. And that meant anyone close to him could be in danger—as the events of last New Year's Eve had proven all too clearly.

But how to explain that to Sky without admitting how broken he truly was? How could he tell her the truth when he knew that the truth would result in losing her? Because while he wasn't prepared to let himself get too attached to the sexy bartender, he also wasn't ready to let her go just yet.

But this time, when he walked back into the bedroom, she was already halfway dressed.

He was admittedly relieved that he wouldn't have to nudge her on her way—and maybe also just the teensiest bit disappointed.

Still, he felt as if he should say something.

This was fun?

Thanks for coming?

Maybe we can do this again sometime?

While he was trying to figure out what that something might be, her cell phone chimed.

Jake glanced at the clock on his bedside table and frowned.

Despite the lateness of the hour, Sky didn't seem surprised by the communication. And after texting a quick reply, she tucked her phone into the back pocket of those snug-fitting jeans.

"This was fun," she said, combing her fingers through her hair and pulling it back to secure it with a ponytail holder. "But I have to go."

Chapter Seven

Jake could hardly protest that Sky was rushing off when he needed her to leave, but he was also curious about where she was going, because he was almost certain it wasn't home.

"Do you need me to drive you somewhere?" he asked, as he pulled on his jeans.

She held up her keys. "I've got my car."

"Have you had your engine checked since you ran out of gas?"

She brushed a light kiss on his lips. "Go back to bed, Jake."

Instead, he followed her through the kitchen to the side door. Molly—who'd been banished from the bedroom again—jumped up from the sofa and joined them, her tail wagging.

Sky slid her feet into her low-heeled boots, then crouched to give the dog a scratch behind the ears.

"Will you text me when you get home?" he asked her.

"No."

He frowned. "Why not?"

"Because we don't have that kind of relationship," she pointed out, in a matter-of-fact tone.

"What kind of relationship do we have?" he wondered.

Which, even as the words left his mouth, he realized was exactly the kind of question that would have made him duck and cringe if she'd asked it.

"Is this really a conversation you want to have at—" she turned her wrist to check the time on her watch "—two thirty-seven in the morning?"

No.

In fact, it was a conversation he knew they weren't ready to have at all. But once again, his brain and his mouth seemed to be having a communication problem because he said, "It seems as good a time as any."

Sky shook her head. "Good night, Jake."

Then she walked out and closed the door, leaving Jake on the other side, scowling.

As a man who closely guarded his own secrets, he could hardly demand to know all of hers.

It was none of his business who'd been texting her in the middle of the night, and yet, he couldn't deny that he felt a little uneasy not knowing where she was going or who she was meeting.

Keep your eyes and ears open at all times. Anything can happen, anywhere. If you realize you've let your guard down, it's already too late.

Except that this wasn't Mosul or Kandahar—this was sleepy little Haven, Nevada in the glorious U S of A and he needed to stop jumping at shadows.

There was no reason for him to worry.

So he went back to bed, but he didn't fall asleep.

What if she ran out of gas again and ended up stranded in the dark?

She'd assured him that she wasn't in the habit of ignoring her car's low-fuel warning, and he had no reason not to believe her. Besides, if she had any kind of trouble, she had her cell phone to call for help— her father or one of her brothers, probably.

She wouldn't call him because, as she'd pointed out, they didn't have that kind of relationship.

And because they'd never exchanged numbers.

Bodily fluids, yes; contact information, no.

He knew where she worked and where she lived, but he didn't know how to get in touch with her if he just wanted to say hi or maybe even ask her to go out sometime.

And yeah, thinking about it now, he realized that he probably should ask her out on a real date sometime.

But where would they go? What would they do?

And how had he jumped from being resigned that they'd never have a relationship to wanting to take the first step toward building one? Especially when just thinking about the possibility made him sweat.

Molly hopped up onto the mattress beside him, nudging his arm with her nose. Because even without a piece of paper, she was capable of reading and responding to his moods. And she added light to his darkest days.

He lifted a hand to stroke her soft fur. "It's okay, girl."

She settled in, resting her chin on his chest.

"What do you think?" he asked her now. "Should I ask Sky to go out with me? Dinner in a restaurant doesn't seem so scary," he decided. "I should be able to handle that, don't you think?"

Molly wagged her tail.

"Do you think she'll say yes? Or do you think she's already figured out that I wasn't exaggerating when I told her my life was seriously screwed up?"

Her tail continued to wave back and forth.

"That's not very helpful, you know," he told her.

She inched further up on the mattress, so that she could swipe at his chin with her tongue.

"Maybe I should just accept the status quo," he continued. "Because you and me have a pretty good thing going here, don't we? Quiet roads for long morning runs, lots of open space for throwing and fetching. We eat when we want, we sleep when we want—or when we can," he acknowledged. "We don't have to worry about anyone's schedule but our own. We don't need to invite a woman into our lives to mess with all that."

And yet, as he finally drifted off to sleep with

Molly beside him, he was starting to think that he wanted one.

But not just anyone.

He wanted Sky.

Sky cranked up the radio and sang along at the top of her lungs as she drove through the darkness of night to the urgent care center on the south side of town. The music kept her focused, so that she didn't drive herself crazy trying to figure out what was going on with Jake—or speculate about what the situation might be when she arrived at her destination.

The message from the supervisor at the women's shelter had been brief, asking only if she was available to visit a patient at the local urgent care clinic. When she'd responded in the affirmative, Deirdre had told her to reach out to Jenny Taft when she got there.

The name sounded vaguely familiar to Sky, but she didn't immediately recognize her former classmate when she walked into the exam room after clearing her visit with the doctor on duty. It wasn't just the bruises and the swelling that distorted the young woman's features, it was the flatness of her blue gaze—a complete absence of life that used to sparkle in the former homecoming queen's eyes when she was Jenny Reashore, before she'd married third-string quarterback Darren Taft.

"Sky," Jenny said, obviously having no similar difficulty recognizing or remembering. "What are you doing here?"

"I'm here to see you," she replied.

"Why?"

She lowered herself into the plastic chair beside the bed. "Because I'm a part-time counselor at April's House, a nearby shelter for abused women and children," she explained, in case the name was unfamiliar to Jenny. "I thought you might want to talk to someone about what happened to you tonight."

The other woman looked away. "I don't think I need to talk to someone about falling down the stairs."

"Okay," Sky said, taking her cue from the patient. "We can talk about anything you want."

"I don't want to talk. I don't even know why I'm still here." Jenny winced as she pushed herself up on the bed. "I need to get dressed. I need to get home."

"I don't think you should go anywhere until the doctors have a chance to review all your test results," Sky cautioned.

"I'm fine," Jenny insisted.

"You're not fine," she said, her tone gentle but firm. "You've got numerous bruises and contusions, three cracked ribs and a probable concussion."

Tears filled Jenny's eyes as she listened to Sky inventory the extent of her injuries. "Darren meant to fix the railing," she said. "He warned me to be careful going downstairs, but I had my arms full of laundry and my foot slipped and…" She started to shrug, then sucked in a pained breath as the movement strained her damaged ribs.

There were all kinds of reasons that women—and men—stayed in abusive relationships. But Sky also knew that sometimes, even when they wanted to leave, they were afraid to take that step, their fear of the unknown even greater than their fear of the abusive partner. Part of her job was to make sure they knew there were options.

But if Jenny wasn't even willing to acknowledge that her husband had hurt her, there wasn't really anything Sky could do to help her. Still, she felt compelled to try one more time. "Are you sure you're telling me everything that happened?"

"I'm sure," Jenny insisted.

"Okay," Sky relented. "And where was Darren when you fell?"

"At work."

"Where does he work?"

"What does that have to do with anything? I slipped and fell down the stairs," she said again.

"Is that what he told you to say?"

Jenny closed her eyes, to hide the tears that welled up again. "Darren loves me."

"Love shouldn't leave bruises—on your body or your spirit," she said.

"I fell. And Dr. Beaudoin had no business suggesting anything different."

"The doctor didn't call April's House," Sky told her.

"Then who did?" Jenny wanted to know.

"Your mom."

This time, when the tears came, Jenny didn't try to hold them back.

* * *

No matter how many times he told himself it was none of his business or concern, Jake couldn't stop wondering about the late-night text message Sky had received. As he went through the usual routines of his day, unanswered questions continued to nag at the back of his mind.

He spent most of the afternoon in the yard with Molly, cutting the grass and raking the clippings. He even pulled weeds from the flowerbeds, all in the hope that Ashley might happen by with Rey, giving him the perfect opening to casually ask the teen how her sister was doing.

But the day faded away with no sign of Ashley or her dog.

As he watched the sun dip in the sky, its light reflecting off the barn windows, he remembered that the caulk around the frames was cracked and peeling. Which meant that he'd have to make a trip to the hardware store soon to get supplies to fix the problem.

Since he was thinking about it now, he might as well go, he decided. And if he was thirsty after he finished running his errand, then it would be perfectly reasonable to stop at Diggers' for a drink before heading home again.

He was feeling quite pleased with himself and the whole scenario he'd planned out—until he walked into the local watering hole and discovered a stranger in Sky's usual place behind the bar.

This bartender was about six feet tall with wide

shoulders and a nose that looked like it had been broken several times. He wore a knit golf shirt with the
Diggers' logo and the name Duke stitched beneath.

"What can I get for you?" Duke asked.

Jake hesitated, uncertain of his next move and
unwilling to acknowledge his deep disappointment.
"Coffee," he decided.

The bartender filled a mug from the carafe on the
warmer. Then he grabbed a caddy filled with sugar
packets and creamers from beside the coffee maker
and set it down beside Jake's cup.

"Thanks."

Duke nodded and moved to the other end of the
bar.

"Coffee's a lot better at The Daily Grind," the customer sitting a couple seats over remarked.

Jake had seen him at the bar a couple of times
before and thought he remembered Sky calling him
Ellis.

"Maybe," Jake allowed.

Undoubtedly, he amended, after taking the first
sip of coffee that was entirely too strong and a little
bit stale.

"But I figured the customers were more likely to
mind their own business here."

"Or maybe you came in looking for Sky," the
other man suggested.

Jake lifted the mug to his lips, not bothering to
respond. He certainly wasn't willing to confide his
motives to this stranger.

"She doesn't work here on Thursdays."

The "here" implying to Jake that she had another job somewhere else.

He reluctantly swallowed another mouthful of coffee. "I didn't ask."

"No, you didn't," Ellis acknowledged. "But I thought you might be wondering."

"Nope," he lied. "I was just running errands and wanted a cup of coffee."

The other man shrugged and turned his attention back to his beer.

Jake left some money on the bar beside his cup, still half full.

As he drove toward home, he cursed himself for not even considering the possibility that he might trek all the way into town and she might not be there.

But at least he had the caulk he needed to fix the windows.

"Christ, it's hot as hell out here," Moore grumbled, sweat dripping down his face as he sprawled on his back under the camouflage cover.

"Thanks, Captain Obvious," Lopez drawled.

The point man saluted. "My pleasure, Major Sarcasm."

"That's because we're in hell," Jake said. "And it's not Captain but Lance Corporal Obvious. Don't be giving him a promotion he hasn't earned or a rank he can't."

A couple of the men chuckled. Most were too hot and irritable to manage more than weak smiles.

"It's not really hell but purgatory," Baker said.

"And heaven is waiting for us all back in the U S of A."

"Doesn't mean we're ever gonna get there," Lucey pointed out.

"We'll get there," Lopez said, needing to believe it. "We just have to survive ten more weeks in this godforsaken dust bowl."

"Nine weeks and six days," Walker corrected.

"But who's counting?" Jake asked dryly.

Of course, they were all counting. Because as proud as they were to serve their country, as deeply as they believed in their mission, no one really wanted to be stuck in the desert, more than seven thousand miles away from their families and friends.

Well, no one except maybe Lance Corporal Brian Lucey, who'd enlisted as soon as he turned eighteen, because the possibility of getting his balls blown off by an IED was preferable to the certainty of being pummeled by his father's fists.

And while the prospect of seeing real action had seemed exciting when they geared up for their deployment, the reality of it had quickly dimmed the shine of their expectations.

But it was the assistant radio officer who spoke up now to say, "I'm counting. 'Cause me and Kelli-Lynn are gonna get married when I get back."

"Hell, Lopez, why would you go and do something like that?" Moore wanted to know.

"'Cause after almost ten months here, marriage doesn't seem quite as terrifying anymore."

"You just want to put a ring on her finger before

she realizes that she can do a lot better than you," Walker said.

Moore snorted and offered a fist bump to the RO.

"I'd rather risk my life than my heart," Moore insisted.

"We do that every day," Lopez pointed out. "And having a wife at home means I'm guaranteed to get laid on homecoming."

"You only need a uniform for that," Baker told him.

They were all laughing when—

Jake jolted awake, his breath coming in short, shallow gasps, his chest tight.

Just a dream.

But it felt *so* real.

Even now, he could hear the echo of the blast ringing in his ears. The wailing sirens. The piercing screams.

"Concentrate on your breathing. Deep breaths. In and out through your mouth.

"Let the air fill your chest...hold it there...then slowly let it out again."

With the doctor's words echoing in his head, Jake silently counted to four as he drew oxygen into his lungs, held it for a count of one, then exhaled to another count of four.

He felt a nudge against his side as he drew in another laboring breath. He lifted his arm and Molly immediately moved in to snuggle close.

Her warm presence immediately soothed him, chasing away the lingering remnants of the dream.

Or had it been a flashback?

He was never entirely sure. Some of the details were indelibly imprinted in his mind, snippets of conversations clearly remembered.

But the blast hadn't happened then. Not like that.

They'd been on their way to a recon post when their Humvee was taken out by an RPG.

Not that he remembered the event or much else about that day. And he wasn't sure if it was a blessing or a curse that the brain trauma he'd suffered had wiped it from his memory.

All he had left were pieces and fragments that his subconscious mind tried to put back together—usually in his dreams.

Molly nudged him again.

"You want to go for a run?"

She leaped off the bed, ready to go.

"All right," he conceded. "But let me put some clothes on first."

By the time he'd pulled on a pair of shorts and a T-shirt and brushed his teeth, she was waiting at the door, quivering with anticipation.

When they'd first moved to Haven, he'd put her on a leash whenever they were out, worried that she might take off after a rabbit or something and not be able to find her way back. But she hated the leash and, after almost tripping him up more than a few times—on purpose, he had no doubt—he'd relented.

And she'd rewarded his trust by never venturing too far from his side.

He opened the front door and she bolted through

it, in case he might doubt how eager she was to get going. But she waited patiently while he locked up and turned the knob to test that it was secure. He was probably the only homeowner in Haven who bothered with such precautions, but most of the other residents had lived there for generations and knew all their neighbors.

Another reason he wasn't sure that country living was for him, though he'd admittedly slept better since he'd made the move three-and-a-half months earlier. It was still rare for him to sleep through to sunrise. If he got four or five hours, he considered that a good night. More important to Jake, the nightmares that had plagued him since everything went to hell in Iraq were less frequent and less intense— this morning's episode notwithstanding.

Of course, that might just be a normal part of the healing process and unrelated to his change of address, he acknowledged, as he jogged toward the road, Molly by his side.

And while it was certainly progress, it wasn't enough.

Almost three years after his discharge from the Marine Corps, he still didn't have a plan for his future.

Without the military, he'd been at a complete loss. Drifting. Unfocused.

He'd started to study communications in college, confident that those skills would be in demand in the private sector if he ever decided to leave the military. But when Luke had deployed to Afghanistan to fight the Taliban, Jake had packed up his books and enlisted, eager to join his brother in the fight for freedom and justice.

He'd thought he might go back to college eventually and finish the degree he'd abandoned. But he hadn't anticipated that the headaches, a less frequent but still lingering side effect of the trauma, would make it difficult for him to stare at a computer screen for long periods of time.

"What are you going to do with your life now?"

Major William Robert Kelly asked the same question every time Jake went home.

And his reply to his father's question was always the same: *"I don't know."*

Because what could he do when everything he'd known and wanted had been taken away from him? His career was over and his other job prospects were dim; his fiancée had jilted him for one of his best friends; and he couldn't even be in a crowd of people without starting to sweat.

"Well, you better figure it out." Not a suggestion so much as an order. *"You can't sit around for the rest of your life."*

Barbara Kelly would attempt to intercede on her son's behalf, her patient and gentle tone a marked contrast to her husband's brusque demands. *"He just needs some time."*

"It's been six months," the Major would grumble.

And then, six months later, *"It's been a year."*

And another six months after that, *"It's been a year and a half."*

Because eighteen months should have been long enough to put the shattered pieces of his life back together.

But every time they had the same conversation, Jake was reminded again that he was a failure—his medical discharge an unsightly stain on the otherwise pristine fabric of the Major's reputation. Because Jake wasn't already distraught enough about the lack of any kind of direction for his future.

"You could reenlist," the Major would offer as a suggestion. *"There would be waivers required, but I know people who could help move things along."*

As if he was unaware of the process.

As if he hadn't already looked into the possibility.

"No!" his mom would immediately protest, her tone no longer so patient or gentle, her eyes filled with tears. *"Dammit, Bill, hasn't he been through enough? He doesn't need you putting those kinds of ideas in his head."*

"He doesn't seem to have any of his own in there."

A frustrating truth that would force an exasperated Jake to confess, "I don't have a lot of anything but ringing in my head these days."

"I thought you said the symptoms were going away." His mother again, immediately concerned.

"Going away doesn't mean gone."

And so it went, every time Jake and his father got into a discussion about his life.

But over the past few months, he'd finally stopped feeling bad that he'd disappointed his father.

Mostly.

And while he hated knowing that his mother continued to worry, there was nothing he could do about that. No matter how many times he told her that he was fine, she refused to believe him.

Of course, she'd always had an uncanny ability to know when he was lying.

Chapter Eight

By the time they hit the mile and a half mark, Jake was feeling a lot better. He signaled to Molly to turn around and head back. As they neared the house, he slowed to a jog, already thinking about breakfast.

The dog had more stamina than he did, and at this point she usually raced ahead to the door, eager for her morning bowl of kibble.

Today she ran past the door and into the backyard.

He stopped and fisted his hands on his hips, gulping air into his lungs. "What do you think you're doing?"

She turned to look at him, obviously wanting him to follow.

"Go on and chase rabbits, if you want," he told her. "But I'm hungry."

She whined, her big brown eyes imploring.

He sighed. "You want to play with Rey, don't you? I'm glad you've made a new friend, but I doubt that Ashley's out with her pup in the morning on a school day."

Molly wagged her tail as she trotted closer to the split-rail fence that bordered the Ferguson property—likely designed to keep the Circle G cattle on their own property more than anything else. It certainly wasn't effective at keeping his dog out.

"If you saw a rabbit, you might as well give up now, because you'll never catch it."

Molly was undeterred, though she paused at the fence, as if waiting for him to catch up. But she didn't wait long before she sidled under the lowest rail and popped up on the other side.

"That's Mr. Gilmore's land and you're trespassing," he told her.

Actually, according to the lawyer, it was his land, but currently subject to a lease agreement with the Circle G.

Molly just wagged her tail.

He turned and started back toward the house, confident that she would fall into step with him. As tempted as she might be by rabbits or squirrels or even the possibility of finding Rey, her first loyalty was to the man who put kibble in her bowl.

But she didn't follow.

Instead, she barked.

He stared her down. "Come."

She didn't come.

"I'm not chasing after you," he said. "I've already run three miles today and I want my breakfast."

Of course, his reasoning did nothing to persuade her.

In obedience classes, he'd been taught to encourage compliance with the command by grabbing her collar and tugging to draw her toward him while repeating the word so that she learned its meaning. But he had to catch her first.

"Molly, come," he said, his tone firm.

She barked again.

Muttering under his breath, Jake marched over to the fence.

"I'm going to call that obedience school and ask for my money back," he grumbled as he climbed over the rail.

Molly, confident that he would follow, headed off through the tall grass.

"I've heard that some ranchers in these parts shoot first and ask questions later," he called out, as he followed her path to a clearing near a copse of trees. "You better hope Mr. Gilmore isn't one of them."

"He's not…usually."

He stopped abruptly when he realized Sky was sitting with her back against one of the trees, her legs stretched out in front of her.

"And my stepmother dragged him off to the antique and craft market today anyway, so no worries on that front today."

He suspected that Molly had somehow known Sky

was there, that she was the reason his dog had been so insistent on breaching the barrier.

And the dog was right now being rewarded for her obstinacy and disobedience with Sky's attention. Of course, Molly was totally lapping it up, sprawled on her back with her legs splayed to afford easy access to her belly for rubbing.

He shook his head. "You are such a slut."

Sky's head tipped back. "Excuse me?"

Luckily she sounded more amused than offended by his remark.

"I didn't mean—I meant—Molly. I was talking to the dog," he said, stumbling through the explanation.

The hint of a smile played at the corners of her mouth. "I can't believe it—you're actually blushing."

He scowled. "I am not."

"I was talking about the dog," she deadpanned.

"So much for man's best friend," he muttered.

Molly basked in the attention of her new friend, unrepentant.

"You've been out running," Sky guessed.

"Oh. Yeah," he admitted, suddenly aware of the sweaty T-shirt stuck to his body. "We were on our way back when Molly decided that she wanted to go exploring rather than go home."

Sky lifted her hand to shield her eyes from the glare as her gaze skimmed over him. "I didn't know you were a runner."

He shrugged. "It's not who I am, it's just something that I do." He dropped onto the grass beside her, so that she didn't have to stare up at the sun. "So…how are you?"

"I'm okay," she said.

"So why are you sitting in the middle of an empty field all by yourself?"

"It's where I come to think sometimes."

"Are you thinking about anything in particular?" he asked.

"Actually, just before you showed up, I was thinking about breakfast."

"Coincidentally, that was my thought, too— before Molly took off," he confided. "Do you want to come over to my place for bacon and eggs?"

"Are you cooking?"

He nodded. "Breakfast is my specialty."

"In that case, yes," she decided.

Molly sat nearby, her focus on Jake at the stove as he pushed strips of bacon around in the pan. Sky was at the table, a cup of coffee in her hands, watching with amusement as the dog watched the man.

"Is there any chance that she's going to get a taste of what you're cooking?" she asked.

"No," Jake said. "But she's an eternal optimist."

"Well, that's at least nicer than what you called her earlier—assuming that you were, in fact, talking about the dog."

"I *was* talking about the dog," he insisted. "Because she'll roll over and spread her legs for anyone in exchange for a belly rub."

"Still, maybe we should talk about what happened with us," she said.

"Why?" he asked warily.

"Because I don't want you to think that I would have gone home with anyone who stopped to fill my gas tank—or waited for me in the parking lot outside Diggers' after work."

"I don't think that," he said.

"But you don't know, do you? Because you really don't know anything about me, despite the fact that anyone in town would be more than happy to fill in the details—real or imagined—if you asked even one question."

"I try to mind my own business."

"Because you don't want other people shoving their noses into yours," she guessed.

He just shrugged.

Not that Sky needed any more of an acknowledgement. And while she was frustrated by his continued reluctance to open up to her, she had to believe that his offer to feed her was at least a step in the right direction.

"Is there anything I can do to help?" she asked him now.

"Cooking bacon and eggs isn't really a two-person job," he told her.

"I could make toast," she offered.

"Except that I didn't get to Battle Mountain this week for groceries, so I don't have any bread," he said.

"You do know there's a grocery store in town, don't you?"

"Yes, I know there's a grocery store in town," he confirmed. "I just prefer to do my shopping in the city."

"The prices are probably a little cheaper at the supermarket," she acknowledged. "But the cost of gas to get there would cancel out any savings." She sipped her coffee. "Or maybe you don't go to Battle Mountain just to save a few bucks."

He didn't respond to that, except to say, "You can check the freezer. There might be a couple of English muffins in there."

She opened the door and discovered the space filled with frozen pizzas and prepackaged microwaveable meals, ice-cream bars and yes, a partial bag of English muffins.

Sky untied the package, took out two muffins, then tied it up again and returned it to the freezer.

"Toaster's in that cupboard," Jake told her, pointing with the spatula.

"Based on the contents of your freezer, I'm guessing that you don't do a lot of cooking, aside from bacon and eggs," she remarked, as she set the appliance on the counter and plugged it in.

"Not a lot," he agreed. "Though I'm a gourmet when it comes to cooking frozen pizza."

"Jamie Oliver better watch his back," she said, tongue in cheek.

"Who?" he asked.

She chuckled softly. "And considering the stack of frozen pizza boxes, I'm going to assume that you have yet to discover Jo's."

"Actually, I've had Jo's pizza a couple of times." He lifted the bacon out of the pan and put it on a paper towel to absorb the grease.

"A couple of times?" she echoed.

He nodded as he cracked eggs over the pan.

"How long have you been in Haven?"

"Almost three months."

"And you know about Jo's but you've only had the best pizza in the known universe, conveniently located on Main Street in this very town, twice?"

"The best pizza in the known universe?" he echoed dubiously.

"You don't agree?"

"It was good," he acknowledged.

"Good?" Her tone was incredulous. "French macarons are good. Swiss cheese is good. Jo's pizza is a culinary masterpiece. If I had to pick only one food to eat for the rest of my life, it would be Jo's pizza."

"It's good pizza," he said again, reaching into the cupboard beside the stove for a couple of plates.

At the same time, the toaster popped, forcing Sky to turn her attention to buttering the muffins.

As Jake plated the bacon and eggs, she found the cutlery drawer and set forks and knives on the table.

"Juice?" he asked, taking a jug from the fridge.

She held up her mug of coffee. "No, this is fine, thanks."

He poured a glass for himself, then joined her at the table.

"How are they?" he asked, after she'd sampled the first bite.

"Really good," she said, lifting another forkful to her mouth.

Jake focused on his own breakfast then. He was mopping up the yolk on his plate with the last bite of English muffin before he said, "I stopped in at Diggers' last night, after a quick trip to the hardware store."

"I'm surprised you didn't go to the hardware store in Battle Mountain," she said, only half teasing.

"So I guess you don't work on Thursdays," he said, pointedly ignoring her cheeky remark.

"Did you go into Diggers' looking for me?" she asked, both surprised and pleased by the possibility.

"I just thought, since I was in town, that I'd say hi."

"Now I'm almost sorry I wasn't there," she said. "But I only work a couple shifts a week."

"So what do you do with the rest of your time?" he wondered.

"Careful," she warned. "Asking questions about my life might lead to a quid pro quo."

"I'm willing to take my chances," he decided.

"Then I'll tell you that the rest of my time is split between my other jobs, spending time with my family and friends and playing coed softball with the Diggers during the summer."

"What's your other job?"

"I think it's my turn to ask a question now," she said and paused, considering. "I'll start with an easy one—are you going to eat that last slice of bacon?"

"What?"

"I'll take that as a no," she said, and snagged it from his plate.

"That was your question?"

She nodded as she bit into the crispy meat. "Your turn again."

"Okay," he said, obviously relieved that she hadn't ventured into personal territory. "Tell me about your other job."

"I'm a youth counselor at the local high school."

"A counselor helps kids pick out their courses and figure out what colleges to apply to, right?"

"That's a guidance counselor," she said. "My job is to give them tools and strategies to deal with stuff like cyberbullying and sexual harassment and drug and alcohol abuse."

"That's heavy stuff," he noted.

She nodded. "And the adolescent years can be particularly challenging ones, so it's crucial that teens know there's someone they can talk to, in confidence, whenever they need to."

"Even if it's two o'clock in the morning?"

"Even if," she agreed.

"Is that why you were in such a hurry to leave here the other night?"

"I was planning to leave, anyway," she pointed out. "But no, the text message was from a nearby women's shelter where I volunteer."

"Apparently you have a much busier schedule than I realized."

"Too busy sometimes," she acknowledged.

"So why don't you cut back on your hours? Or even give up one of the jobs?" he suggested.

She shrugged. "I only have office hours at the high school two days a week, although sometimes I get called in at the request of a student or to address a specific issue. And I usually spend a few hours at April's House on the weekends, but I'll also go in during the week if the shelter is busy."

"And Diggers'?"

"I'm there every Wednesday and Friday and every other Sunday," she said. "The late hours take a toll sometimes, but I really enjoy the interactions with customers. The Daily Grind might be popular for hot coffee and hotter gossip, but Diggers' is the heart of the community. It's where people gather for a drink after work or to grab a bite with friends or to celebrate all the big and little milestones in their lives.

"In three years, I've seen a lot of milestones, though there are still people who don't approve of me working there," she confided.

"Like your father?" he guessed.

She frowned. "How'd you know that?"

"Ashley mentioned it."

"When were you talking to my little sister?"

He shrugged. "She brings Rey over when she's bored."

"Then she must be here a lot," Sky decided. "Because she's *always* bored. And it's going to be even worse when school's out for the summer."

"Because most of her friends live in town," Jake

noted, obviously echoing one of her sister's common complaints.

"It was no different for me when I was growing up," Sky pointed out. "Although I had a sister and two brothers, so I was never really alone—even when I wanted to be."

"Forced proximity makes convenient playmates."

"Sounds like you speak from experience," she said.

"I have a brother," he told her. "Luke. He's four years older than me."

"Where did you grow up?"

"Here and there."

"Military brats, huh? Is your dad a Marine, too?" At his questioning look, she shrugged. "Even in the dark, that tattoo on your shoulder is hard to miss."

"Yeah," he finally said. "My dad's a major in the US Marine Corps."

She didn't know a lot about military structure, but she knew that major was a pretty high rank.

Jake gathered up their plates and pushed away from the table, a clear indication that the topic of conversation was closed.

"Do you want me to give you a ride home?" he asked.

"No, I can walk," she said. "I just didn't expect to be kicked out *before* we had sex this time."

He seemed taken aback by her response.

"I invited you to come over for breakfast because I didn't want you to think that all I wanted from you was sex," he said.

"Are you saying that you don't want to have sex?"

"Men pretty much always want to have sex," he told her.

"And yet, I've been here—" she glanced at the watch on her wrist "—more than an hour, and you haven't even kissed me."

"It's been a concerted effort to keep my hands off you," he promised.

"I like when your hands are on me."

"Good to know, but—" he held them up now and took a step back "—I was actually thinking we might try something different next time."

"What do you mean by different?" she asked, her tone wary.

"I mean like going out for dinner."

"We just had breakfast and you're already thinking about dinner?" she teased.

"I wasn't necessarily suggesting tonight."

Her pretty blue-grey eyes sparkled. "Are you asking me on a date, Jake Kelly?"

"Yes, I'm asking you on a date, Sky Gilmore," he confirmed, parroting her with a smile.

"Then I'm saying yes," she told him. "When? Where?"

He wanted to say tonight but since that might come across as too eager, especially considering her remark about their recent meal, he suggested Tuesday instead.

She gave a slight shake of her head. "I can't do dinner on Tuesday," she said, sounding sincerely regretful. "Tuesdays are game nights."

"Game nights?"

"The coed softball team I mentioned—I play third base," she explained.

"The hot corner," he noted, impressed. "You must be good."

"I am," she said, but it was a matter-of-fact statement rather than a boast.

"Okay, so you have baseball on Tuesday and you work on Wednesday, so how about Thursday?"

"Thursday sounds good to me," she agreed.

"Okay, then," he agreed. "We'll do it on Thursday."

"But dinner first, right?" she teased.

He smiled, appreciating not just her humor but the promise implicit in her words. "Definitely dinner first."

Chapter Nine

It was Sky's opinion that one of the best things about not having a regular full-time job was that she was often available whenever a friend or family member needed her. And while she wasn't always thrilled to be enlisted to run errands for the ranch, she never hesitated to step up when Katelyn needed someone to watch Tessa for a couple hours or her sister-in-law Macy asked for help with the triplets.

So on Wednesday afternoon, when Kate called to tell her that she was still stuck in a trial that should have been finished two days earlier, Sky happily agreed to take Tessa to her Tadpole lesson at the community center. The swimming class was made up of a small group of toddlers who, along with their parents or caregivers, were taught water safety and foundational skills.

Tessa's favorite part was when she got to be a starfish, spreading her arms and legs wide and floating on top of the water with her aunt's hand supporting her back. She was less enamored of the putting-her-face-in-the-water part.

When the class was finished, Sky and Tessa returned to the locker room to shower—"We hafta wash off the kwoween, Auntie 'ky"—and get dressed. Of course, toweling the little girl's head wasn't good enough for Tessa, who insisted on standing beneath the hand dryer until there wasn't a drop of moisture left in her hair.

"I think I understand now why your mom warned me that a half-hour swim class takes two hours," Sky remarked, as she wrapped the wet swimsuits in their towels before tucking them into Tessa's glittery pink backpack. Of course she didn't really mind, because she'd enjoyed every minute of those two hours she'd spent with her adorable niece.

But they weren't done yet. Because on their way to the exit, they had to go right past the library.

"Books! Books!" Tessa insisted.

And there was no way Sky, a lifelong lover of reading herself, could possibly say no to her.

Another half an hour later, they were finally on their way out of the building, with half a dozen books stuffed in the front pouch of Tessa's backpack, away from the damp towels.

Sky held her niece's hand securely in hers as the

little girl carefully navigated the outside steps. As Tessa reached the bottom, Sky caught a glimpse, out of the corner of her eye, of a truck pulling into the parking lot.

Was that… Jake's truck?

She turned her head for a better look, surprised to realize that it was. And even more surprised when his passenger side door opened and a woman got out.

Sky recognized the stunning, statuesque blonde as Natalya Vasilek, an assistant manager at Adventure Village who occasionally came into Diggers' with her coworkers for a drink and a bite to eat. In addition to working at the family-friendly activity center, Natalya was a former naval aviator who organized weekly support group meetings for other military veterans.

As Nat came around the back of the vehicle, Sky saw that she carried a wide flat box from Sweet Caroline's Sweets. Donuts or some other kind of pastries for the meeting, she guessed.

Jake fell into step with the other woman, obviously continuing whatever conversation they'd been having in the car. In fact, he was so focused on what they were talking about, he was almost at the bottom step before he spotted Sky standing there with Tessa.

He stopped abruptly in mid-stride and his lips started to curve, as if he was happy to see her, but the curve didn't quite reach the point of a smile before his gaze shuttered.

"Hi," Sky said, her greeting encompassing both of them.

"Hey, Sky." The other woman's easy response was accompanied by a real smile, even as her gaze shifted from Jake to Sky and back again, curious and assessing.

Jake's response wasn't quite as easy, and Sky realized he wasn't just startled by this chance encounter but maybe a little uncomfortable, too.

Because he was with Nat?

Or because he didn't want her to know that he was going to a support group?

Nat clearly sensed the subtext between them because she gestured to the box she carried. "I'm going to take this inside," she said, and made her escape.

Jake nodded, though his attention never shifted away from Sky.

"I didn't expect—what are you doing here?" he asked, when Nat was out of earshot.

"My sister was stuck in court, so I brought Tessa to her swimming group today," she said.

"I swimmed," her niece said proudly.

His gaze shifted now to the little girl clinging to Sky, and his expression immediately softened. "Do you like swimming?"

Tessa's head bobbed up and down as she released her aunt's hand to reach both arms up into the air and stretch her legs out. "I a 'tarfiss."

"She means starfish," Sky translated.

He nodded. "I've got an almost-three-year-old niece, so I'm pretty fluent in toddler-speak. Plus, the pose," he acknowledged. "Definitely a starfish."

Tessa beamed at him. "An' I got books."

"At the library?" he guessed.

The little girl responded with more head bobbing.

"Sounds like you've both had a busy day."

"And mine is a long way from over," Sky said. "I need to get Tessa home so that I can go home and get ready for work."

Jake nodded. "I'll see you later then?"

She smiled. "I hope so."

Natalya was almost finished arranging the chairs by the time Jake made his way to the usual meeting room.

"I thought I was here to help you set up," he remarked.

"So did I." But her remark was followed by a smile to assure him that she wasn't bothered by his tardiness.

Still, he felt compelled to say, "You could have waited for me."

"I'm perfectly capable of unstacking chairs, Jake. The main reason I asked you to come into town early was because I needed a ride."

And he knew it hadn't been easy for her to ask for even that small favor. Natalya Vasilek was one of the most fiercely independent people he'd ever met, and he suspected that she would have preferred to walk to the community center from home rather than accept a ride, except that she had to pick up the donuts from Sweet Caroline's.

"How long are you going to be without wheels?" he asked her now.

"Just a couple more days—I hope." She finished with the chairs, then moved into the kitchenette to begin making coffee. "It's just frustrating to be inconvenienced by something that wasn't at all my fault."

She'd given him a quick rundown of the situation on the phone, explaining that someone had backed into her car in the parking lot at Adventure Village. What annoyed her even more was that the driver of the other vehicle took off. Thankfully, there were surveillance cameras on the property that recorded the incident, so her car was now being repaired and the other driver's insurance was paying for it.

"Well, I'm generally around," he said now. "If you need me to play chauffeur again."

"Thanks," she said. "But I only tagged you tonight because we were coming to the same place."

"How are you getting to and from work?"

"I've been hitching a ride with a coworker."

"Is this, by any chance, the coworker that you've sort of been seeing?" he asked.

"It might be," she allowed.

"So…things are going well?" he prompted.

"They might be."

He caught the hint of a smile on her face. "Good for you, Nat."

"What's going on with you?" she asked.

It was the same question she asked him every Wednesday, and every Wednesday he gave her the same answer: "Nothing much."

But somehow, over the past several weeks, they'd

become friends. And tonight he actually had something to tell her. Something he wanted—maybe even needed—to talk about. "I've got a date tomorrow night."

"A date," Nat echoed. "That sounds promising."

"Does it? Because I'm already thinking it was a mistake to ask."

"I'd suggest that we save the talking about your feelings and concerns part for the meeting, except that you seem to clam up whenever there are more than three people in the room."

While he wouldn't say that he clammed up, it was true that he didn't share personal insights or anecdotes with the group. He went to the meetings because his doctor had suggested that interacting with others who had similar experiences might help him feel less alone. It did that, and it got him out of the house at least once a week.

"So tell me why you're thinking it was a mistake," Nat suggested now.

"It just seems like a really big step, and I'm not sure that I'm ready."

"So why did you ask her out?"

"Because I want to be ready," he admitted.

"You really like her," she noted.

He nodded. "I really do. But she has no idea how completely screwed up I am."

"So tell her," Nat urged. "Honesty and communication are at the core of any good relationship."

"I've tried to tell her."

"Have you?"

"Well, I started to…but then… I didn't really know what to say. Or maybe I just didn't want to talk about it. I know she has a right to know what she's getting herself into…except that I'm not sure whatever is happening between us is anything. And I'm pretty sure that if she did know, she'd run away—far and fast."

"I don't think you're giving her enough credit. I'd bet that Sky Gilmore can handle whatever you throw at her."

He frowned. "How did you know I was talking about Sky?"

"Please," she said. "I nearly got singed from the heat between the two of you, even standing several feet away."

"Is that all you're going to say about it?"

She flipped the switch to start the coffee brewing. "Are you asking for my approval?"

"How about your opinion?"

"I've always liked Sky," Nat told him.

"You don't think I'm aiming too high?"

"Of course I think you're aiming too high. Sky isn't just beautiful and smart, she's kind and compassionate. She's always ready and able to volunteer for anything that will help the community and happy to give of her time and expertise without expecting anything in return. She is an amazing woman who could no doubt do a lot better than a grumpy old vet like you."

He frowned at that, and Nat smiled before continuing, "I also think she just might be a woman who's capable of understanding and appreciating you, and you deserve no less."

That night, Jake wasn't waiting for Sky when she left the restaurant. But they'd exchanged contact information over the weekend, and she saw now that he'd sent her a text message.

You want to stop by after work?

The time stamp of that message was 12:37. Then, at 12:41, it was followed up with:

If you're not too tired.

Just the thought of seeing Jake again seemed to magically lift away the weariness of the long day. *Definitely not too tired.* She tapped a quick reply:

On my way. If it's not too late.

His reply was immediate:

Definitely not too late :)

The smiley face emoji made her smile as she exited the parking lot.

Both Jake and Molly were waiting for her at the door when she arrived. But this time, instead of leaving a trail of clothes on the way to the bedroom, Jake took her hand and led her into the living room.

"Are we trying something different again?" Sky teased.

"As a matter of fact." He lowered himself onto the sofa, then drew Sky down on his lap, and settled his mouth over hers.

His kiss was different this time. A leisurely exploration rather than a means to an end. And if Sky was a little surprised by his restraint, she was more entranced by his technique. As his lips teased and tempted her own, desire raced through her veins like a drug, making her heart race and her blood pound.

Was it possible to become addicted to a man's kisses?

She thought maybe it was, as the more kisses they shared, the more she wanted.

She shifted in his lap, so that her knees were bracketing his hips. So that she could lift her arms to his shoulders, linking her hands behind his head. His arms banded around her, pulling her closer until her breasts were pressed against the firm wall of his chest. Her nipples immediately tightened to hard aching points. Between her thighs, she could feel solid evidence of his arousal, proof that he wanted her, too.

She slid her hands beneath the hem of his shirt, her fingers gliding over his warm, taut skin, instinctively gentling as they skimmed the jagged scar that ran from just above his hip almost to his armpit.

Jake caught her wrists and pulled her hands away.

"It's hard to remember that I'm trying to take things slow when you're touching me," he told her.

She was glad to hear his breathing was labored, because she needed a moment to catch her own breath before she could respond. "Isn't it a little late to start taking things slow?"

"I know this seems a bit backward," he acknowledged. "But I want to get to know you—and for you to know me, so that you know what you're getting into."

She narrowed her gaze. "It sounds like you're dumping me."

"No!"

Sky was somewhat appeased by his quick and vehement denial.

"Though truthfully, I didn't expect that you'd want to have anything more to do with me after that first day," he confided to her now.

"You're referring to the day you told me to get out after we'd mated like bunnies?" she teased.

"I didn't say 'get out,'" he denied. "But yes, when you were willing to give me another chance after that, I knew you were truly unlike any other woman I've ever known."

"Good," she said. "I hate to be predictable."

"Does that mean you're not going to barrage me with questions?" he asked, sounding both skeptical and relieved.

"I'll try to limit my inquiries to a trickle," she promised. "But questions about what exactly?"

"Why I was at the community center with Natalya."

"Oh. I assumed that you were both there for the veterans' support group meeting."

He frowned at that.

"Was I wrong?" she asked.

"No," he admitted.

"So why do I get the impression that you're disappointed by my response?"

"I'm not disappointed, I'm just…surprised," he realized. "Margot would sulk if I so much as smiled at another woman."

"Now I have a barrage of questions," Sky said, leaning back a little to better see his face. "Starting with—who's Margot?"

He winced. "You're so easy to talk to that sometimes I forget to filter the words that come out of my mouth."

"And yet you're not answering the question," she noted.

"Margot was…my fiancée."

"Oh." She took a moment to consider this revelation. "I didn't realize you'd been engaged."

He shrugged. "It feels like it was a lifetime ago."

"How long ago was it really?" she pressed.

"She gave back the ring about two years ago."

"How long did she wear it?"

His brows drew together, as if he was trying to remember. "Almost five years?"

"That's a pretty lengthy engagement," she noted.

"Yeah," he agreed.

"Did you have a date set for a wedding?"

He shook his head. "During those five years, I was gone more than I was home. It was hard enough to commit to a night out with friends, forget planning the kind of wedding she wanted."

"But you did want to marry her." It was a statement more than a question, as Sky tried to wrap her head around the fact that this taciturn man had been planning a happily-ever-after.

"Sure," he said. "I mean, my focus was on the Marine Corps, but I looked forward to coming home from a deployment and seeing her face in the crowd. To know that there was someone there for me. My parents always came to the homecomings, too, but everyone's parents were always there. Having a pretty girl waiting was something special."

She didn't miss that he'd said "a pretty girl" rather than use his fiancée's name, making Sky wonder if he'd truly been in love with the woman who'd worn his ring or if he'd just wanted to feel connected to someone back home. Or maybe she was reading too much into his word choice, because she didn't want to think that the man she was starting to fall for had fallen for someone else, even if that relationship was long over.

"So what went wrong?" she asked him now.

"It turned out that she loved the idea of being with a man in uniform more than she loved me. And when I no longer wore the uniform, she found someone else. Actually…she found him before I got my discharge papers."

"Hence your comment about Molly being more loyal than any woman you've ever known," she realized, aware that it couldn't have been an easy admission for him to make, and glad he felt comfortable enough with her to share the whole truth of his failed relationship.

"Yeah. I guess I'm having a little trouble forgiving Margot for that," he acknowledged.

"Do you think you should forgive her?"

He shrugged. "I don't think it's okay that she cheated, but I understand that I was no longer the man she'd fallen in love with."

"Love endures all things," Sky said.

"If you're such an expert on the subject, what are you doing here with me?" he wondered.

"I'm only an expert at looking for love in all the wrong places," she confided.

"That would explain it," he said.

"You don't have to worry," she assured him. "I'm not looking for anything more than what we've found between us."

"It's good, isn't it?" he asked, the hint of a smile curving his lips.

"Very good," she agreed, and kissed him again.

Sky couldn't remember the last time she'd been out on a date. Hanging out with a group of friends that included males, sure. But a one-on-one date with a guy she really liked? It had been ages.

"Why are all your clothes on your bed?" Ashley asked, hovering in the doorway of Sky's room.

Looking at the pile of discarded clothes, Sky had to sigh. "Because I can't decide what to wear."

"For what?"

"I've got a date," she confessed.

"I thought you were on a dating hiatus," Ashley said, remembering what Sky had told her when she'd asked why she didn't have a boyfriend. Or girlfriend, she'd been quick to present as another option, to assure her sister that she wouldn't judge.

"I was, but now I'm not."

"So who are you going out with? Is it Jake?"

"Why would you think it was Jake?" Sky asked her.

"Because you've known everyone else in this town forever, so if you wanted to go out with any of them, it would have happened before now," Ashley said.

And probably had, she acknowledged, though she didn't share that with her sister.

"You're right," she said instead. "I'm going out with Jake."

"Where are you going?"

"Just for dinner."

"A casual restaurant or fancy restaurant?"

"I have no idea," she admitted.

"No wonder you can't figure out what to wear," her sister sympathized. "You want to wear something nice, because it's a date, but you don't want to overdress and have him think you're making a bigger deal of the event than it is."

"Insightful commentary from someone who isn't allowed to date yet," Sky remarked.

"Don't remind me," Ashley said, sounding pained. "But I'll be prepared when Dad finally gives the thumbs-up."

Sky held a skirt and top in front of her. "What do you think?"

"I love the skirt." Ashley rifled through a pile of tops on the bed. "But with this top."

Sky swapped the pink one in her hand for the blue from her sister and turned to face her reflection in the mirror. "Hmm...you're right. This one's better."

"So maybe you'll let me borrow this one—" Ashley, still holding the discarded pink top, looked hopeful "—to wear to the movies tonight?"

"Do you have a date?" Sky asked.

Her sister rolled her eyes. "I'm not allowed to date—remember?"

Yeah, Sky remembered.

She also remembered that, when she was Ashley's age, being told she couldn't do something rarely stopped her from doing it.

"So who are you going to the movies with?" she asked.

"Chloe."

"Then you don't need this," Sky said, tugging the shirt out of her sister's hand. "Because Chloe won't care what you're wearing."

"There might be some other people there tonight," Ashley admitted. "I mean, the movie theater's a public place, right?"

"Uh-huh," Sky agreed.

"So if we happen to run into some other people that we know and decide to sit together, there's nothing wrong with that. And even if Chloe specifically invited other people who might be boys, it's still not technically a date, right?"

"Are you asking me or telling me?"

Ashley sighed. "I really didn't care who else was going—I just wanted to see the movie. But then Chloe decided to invite her boyfriend, and then he invited his friend, and now I'm really nervous about going because his friend is really cute and whenever I think about sitting next to him in the theater, I get this quivery feeling in my stomach."

"I agree with Dad that you're kind of young to be dating," she said, handing the pink top back to her sister. "But going to the movies with a few friends shouldn't be taboo."

Ashley rewarded her with a radiant smile. "Thanks. For the top, I mean."

Sky nodded. "Just be smart and be safe—and don't let anyone put their hands under that top."

Her sister looked horrified by the very thought. "I wouldn't... Never," she promised.

Though she was skeptical about the "never" part, Sky felt confident that her sister had established limits for her night at the movies.

"But what if..." Ashley chewed on her bottom lip. "What if he wants...to kiss me?"

"That's entirely up to you," Sky said. "No one else."

"Chloe French kisses her boyfriend," the teen confided now. "She says it's a real turn on, but it sounds pretty gross to me."

"I think you're starting to realize that Chloe does a lot of things you're not comfortable doing, and that's okay. You need to set and respect your own boundaries."

"Do you let Jake put his tongue in your mouth?" Ashley's cheeks turned pink as she asked the question.

Not just his tongue, Sky mused, but she was definitely not going *there* with her little sister.

"I can appreciate that you're curious about some things, and that's perfectly normal and natural," Sky said instead. "But I'm going to keep the details of my private relationships private."

"Have you had sex with him?" Ashley asked, her eyes widening.

"Refer to previous answer."

Her sister huffed out a breath. "Well, it's not like I can talk to mom about this stuff."

Sky perched on the edge of the mattress beside Ashley. "Actually, I bet your mom would be glad to answer your questions—so long as they aren't about the details of what goes on in her bedroom."

"You're right," the teen acknowledged. "It's just that talking to your mom about this stuff is awkward, you know?" Then her eyes went wide and her cheeks colored again as she suddenly realized that her sister didn't know, because Sky's mom had died when she was only seven. "Ohmygod, Sky… I'm *so* sorry."

"It's okay, Ash," she said. "And actually I *do* know, because Grandma tried to have those talks with me—when I got my first period, bought my first bra, went to my first high-school dance. So yes, I understand awkward."

She also remembered that when there was something she really wanted to talk about, in the absence of her mother, she'd naturally turned to her big sister. So maybe she shouldn't have been surprised that Ashley had come to her, even if their relationship was a recent revelation for both of them.

Chapter Ten

Jake was waiting outside when Sky arrived.

"Am I late?" she asked.

"No."

He brushed her lips with a soft, lingering kiss that made her belly quiver in the same way her sister had described.

"I just didn't know what you'd be wearing and I didn't want Molly jumping and messing you up."

She did a quick twirl. "Do I look okay?"

"Better than okay. You look amazing."

"You clean up pretty good yourself," she said, appreciating how handsome he looked in a chambray shirt and khaki pants. "And not a dog hair in sight."

"I would have been happy to pick you up at your place," he said.

"This is easier."

"Because you don't want me to meet your father?" he guessed.

"We're neighbors in a small town—I'd assumed you'd already met my father."

"But not as your date," he remarked.

"And that's what I was trying to save you from," she said. "The interrogation that goes along with that title."

"I know how to handle an interrogation—name, rank and serial number."

She smiled, pleased that he no longer seemed to be keeping his military service a secret—at least not from her.

"Well, I have a question for you," she said. "Where are we going tonight?"

"The Chophouse."

"In Battle Mountain?" she guessed.

He nodded and opened the passenger-side door of his truck for her to climb in.

"There are restaurants in Haven," she reminded him, when he was settled behind the wheel.

"That I can count on the fingers of one hand without using my thumb," he noted. "And of those four, you work at one, your brother owns another, and while the Sunnyside Diner does a great all-day breakfast, I think we've eaten enough eggs together."

"And for some inexplicable reason, you're not a fan of Jo's pizza," she remembered.

"I like it just fine."

"And yet your freezer is full of the frozen kind."

"Maybe because I don't want to go into town every time I'm in the mood for a pizza."

"Definitely worth the trip," Sky argued.

"The first time I had it, I thought the same thing," he agreed.

"And the second?" she prompted.

He sighed. "I walked into the restaurant and before I could even give my name at the takeout counter, the woman working the register—who I assumed to be Jo—said, 'Your medium sausage and peppers is just coming out of the oven now.'"

"It was the wrong order?" Sky guessed.

"No, it was the right order. But I don't need everyone in town knowing what I eat on my pizza."

"And since then you've deprived yourself of Jo's pizza because you'd rather be anonymous than well-fed?"

"It sounds ridiculous when you say it like that," he acknowledged.

"It is ridiculous," she said. "I'll be the first to admit that it's sometimes annoying that everyone seems to know everyone else's business. When you live in a town like Haven, you forfeit your anonymity, but what you get in return is a sense of belonging to the community.

"But I'm willing to make you a deal," she said, as he pulled into the parking lot adjacent to the restaurant.

"What kind of deal?" he asked warily.

"If this date thing goes well enough tonight that

we decide we want to do it again, we'll eat at your place next time—and I'll pick up the pizza from Jo's."

"That sounds good to me," he agreed.

"This is really nice," Sky said, after they'd been seated. The décor had a masculine bent, with lots of stone, wood and leather, with subdued overhead lighting supplemented by candles on the tables. But it was the scent of grilled meat that really appealed to her empty stomach.

"I hoped you'd like it," he said.

"Have you been here before?"

He shook his head. "No, but it had good reviews online."

"What did we do before the internet?" she mused.

"I'm pretty sure we didn't take pictures of our every meal to share with the world."

She chuckled. "I take it you're not a fan of Instagram?"

"I'm not a fan of social media in general," he admitted.

"I'm not surprised," she said, tongue in cheek. "Considering it's got the word *social* in it."

Jake narrowed his gaze, but whatever his intended reply, he bit it back when the waitress appeared beside their table.

"Can I get you something to drink while you're looking at the menu?" she asked. "We have a selection of red and white wines, available by the glass or bottle, a variety of craft beers and an extensive cocktail list."

"Sky?" Jake said, deferring to her.

"I wouldn't mind a glass of wine," she said, skimming the list of options at the front of the menu. "The Stoneridge Estates pinot noir."

The waitress nodded.

"And you, sir?" she asked Jake.

"I'll have a Coke," he said.

Sky continued to peruse the menu offerings, mentally debating between the striploin and ribeye because she didn't believe in going to a steak house and ordering anything but steak. She glanced up to ask Jake what he was going to have, and found his gaze was on her rather than the menu in his own hand.

"You're staring at me," she said.

"I can't help it—you look particularly beautiful tonight."

"I think it's the candlelight," she said.

"No." He shook his head. "It's you."

"And you haven't even been drinking," she said lightly.

"I'm surprised," he said. "You don't strike me as the type of woman who'd have trouble accepting a sincere compliment."

"I don't," she said. "But I grew up with a sister who's truly beautiful. If you'd met Katelyn, you'd understand."

"I have met her. She was my uncle's lawyer."

Sky nodded. "Then you should understand."

"She's very attractive," he acknowledged. "But when I walked into her office, I didn't feel the same kind of awareness I felt when I walked into Diggers' and saw you."

"Lucky for you, considering that Kate's married to the sheriff," she remarked.

When the waitress returned with their drinks and a basket of warm bread, Sky ordered the striploin with a fully loaded baked potato and the seasonal vegetables—broccoli and carrots. Jake opted for the T-bone with the same sides.

"So tell me," Sky said as she buttered a slice of bread, "why a man who, by his own admission, prefers anonymity, would move to a town like Haven."

"I wanted to get out of San Diego and, when I found out that my uncle had put my name on the title before he passed away, it seemed like my best option. Maybe my only option."

"Were you surprised to learn that he'd left this place to you?"

"More than," he confided.

"He never talked to you about it?"

He shook his head. "Although, to be honest, the last time I was here was the summer before I went away to college. No, it was the Christmas holidays during my first year of college. Fifteen years ago." He shifted his gaze to the window. "I didn't even make it back for Anna's funeral because I was…out of the country."

"You mean deployed?"

He nodded.

"Why do you do that?"

"What did I do?"

"Avoid referencing your military service."

He lifted a shoulder. "It's just not something I'm comfortable talking about."

"Do you talk about it in your Wednesday night support group?"

"No," he admitted.

She wished he would talk to her, but she knew this wasn't the time or place to push him for answers to her questions. Instead she asked, "You were close to Ross and Anna?"

He nodded again. "My brother and I used to spend a couple weeks with them every summer when we were kids."

"And yet our paths never crossed back then," she mused.

"I'm glad they crossed now."

"Me, too." Sky smiled, even as she saw the situation developing out of the corner of her eye. The young waiter—his eyes on a pretty girl dining with her family—turning abruptly, directly into the path of a busboy, knocking the bin of glasses that he carried out of his hands.

She had a split second to brace herself, but she didn't think to warn Jake—and didn't know if it would have mattered anyway.

There was a loud crash...

The pressure wave from the blast sent Jake stumbling even before he registered the sound of the boom some distance away. Flying shards of blown-

*out glass flew in every direction, not just dangerous
but potentially lethal—*

"Jake."

*He blinked, trying to focus through the cloud of
dust that filled the room.*

"Jake."

Sky reached across the table and touched a hand
to his arm. "Are you okay?"

He blinked. His nostrils were flared, his breathing shallow.

"Yeah." He swallowed. "I just… Can you give
me a minute?"

"Sure," she said.

He pushed away from the table and walked out
of the restaurant.

Jake couldn't remember the last time he'd been
on a first date with a woman. And as he focused on
inhaling and exhaling to help ward off the impend-
ing panic attack, he acknowledged that his first real
date with Sky Gilmore was also likely to be his last.

*"Triggers can be sights, sounds or scents that
remind you of the trauma. They can happen anytime, anywhere. Quite often they will happen at in-
opportune times and inconvenient places. You need
to learn to recognize the signs and utilize your cop-
ing mechanisms."*

Well, at least he hadn't tackled his date, upended
the table or reached for a weapon that he wasn't carrying.

Was that progress? Should he be proud?

He scrubbed his hands over his face.

What had he been thinking, asking her to go out with him?

The problem was, when he was with Sky, he sometimes had trouble thinking. Or at least remembering all the reasons that he didn't do the things that most normal people did. Because when he was with her, he felt normal. No, he felt invincible, as if he could take on the world with her by his side.

He'd been looking forward to this opportunity for them to spend more time together and get to know one another a little better outside of the bedroom. Because when they were naked and horizontal together, they didn't tend to do a lot of talking. And being with Sky made him want to open up, perhaps for the first time in years. So much so that he'd thought he might be able to tell her things that he'd never told anyone else outside of a doctor's office.

"Jake?"

He heard the tentativeness in her tone. Or maybe it was fear. He could hardly blame her for being scared. Some days he scared himself.

He turned slowly to face her, though she was mostly in shadow.

But she stepped closer now, into the light, and he saw that she wasn't scared but worried.

About him.

"Are you okay?" she asked.

"Yeah," he lied. "Sorry about that."

"There's no reason for you to apologize."

He appreciated the sentiment, but he didn't share it.

"I just need another minute and then I'll meet you back inside."

"Why don't you give me your keys instead?" she suggested.

"Why?"

"So that I can drive us home."

"But…we haven't had dinner yet," he said inanely.

As if there was any chance she'd want to share a meal with him now.

"We'll have it at your place," she said, holding up the takeout bag he hadn't realized she was carrying.

He felt as if a ninety-pound pack had been lifted off his back. The tension in his neck immediately lessened, the tightness in his chest eased.

"Keys?" she prompted.

He dug them out of his pocket and put them into her outstretched hand.

She didn't say anything as she pulled out of the parking lot and turned back toward Haven, and he didn't know what to say.

When they got back to his place, Molly made a big fuss over him, as if he'd been gone for days rather than a couple of hours. Or maybe she knew how much he needed her unwavering love and support, because even when Sky walked in with the doggy bag containing their steaks, Molly didn't move from his side.

"Go into the living room and relax," Sky said. "I'll heat up the food and let you know when it's ready."

"You don't have to do that," Jake said. "I'm sure you'd rather—"

"Go," she said again, pointing toward the living room.

So he went, too exhausted to argue any more.

But he did feel compelled to apologize once more, when their dinner had been reheated and he was seated across from her at the kitchen table.

"I'm sorry. I should have realized it was a bad idea—I did realize it was a bad idea." He stabbed his fork into a broccoli spear. "I picked up the phone to cancel at least half a dozen times."

"But you didn't," she noted, slicing into her steak.

"Because I wanted to prove myself wrong. I wanted to prove that I could at least take a pretty girl to a restaurant and fake being normal for a few hours. Guess that didn't work out so well, did it?"

"How long have you been having panic attacks?"

"A couple of years."

"Have you talked to anyone about what causes them?"

"You mean a shrink?" he guessed.

"I mean a qualified professional," she clarified.

"Aren't you a qualified professional?"

"PTSD isn't my area of expertise," she told him. "Not to mention that sleeping with a patient violates all kinds of rules that would result in my license being revoked. But if there's anything you want to talk about, I'm more than willing to listen."

"I don't know what to say, how to explain something I don't understand, though there were plenty of doctors who made me try."

"Can you tell me what kinds of things trigger a response?" she prompted, her tone encouraging.

He sighed. "Anything. And yet nothing consistently," he admitted, obviously frustrated by the fact. "Sudden noises. Flashes of light."

"I don't imagine the Fourth of July is a lot of fun for you," she said lightly.

"Fireworks are a definite trigger," he confirmed. "As I found out this past New Year's Eve."

"What happened then?"

"I didn't even want to celebrate," he confided. "But it was the first time in several years that both me and my brother were home for the holidays, and my mom insisted that the whole family should be together.

"Luke and his wife Raina offered to host dinner. I was a little uneasy all night—because me and my dad can't be in the same room for too long without butting heads over something, usually the lack of a plan for my future," he acknowledged. "But it was a really nice evening. Raina's not only a fabulous cook, she managed to keep the conversation focused on mostly neutral topics.

"Everything was great until the kids next door lit a handful of cherry bombs. Just kids being kids, right?"

Jake looked off in the distance, his expression bleak.

Sky reached across the table to squeeze his hand, a silent gesture of support.

She didn't need him to tell her the rest of the story. She could see the direction it was going clearly enough to figure out the end for herself. But if Jake was finally ready to talk, she wanted to listen and support him.

To reassure him that he wasn't alone.

"But those pops sounded like gunfire to me," he continued. "And I reacted without thinking. Because in a combat zone, if you think, you're dead, so you learn pretty quickly to take action.

"Benjamin, my nine-year-old nephew, was closest to me, and I threw him to the ground, covering his body with my own." His Adam's apple bobbed as he swallowed. "I thought I was protecting him."

He closed his eyes, but not before she caught a glimpse of both guilt and regret in his anguished gaze.

"Instead, I knocked the wind out of him, scared him half to death—and did a pretty good job of freaking out everyone else, too."

"You thought you were protecting him," she reminded Jake.

"The next day, I went to see my sister-in-law, to apologize for traumatizing her son. I was prepared for her to tell me to stay the hell away from her family—that seemed the most reasonable response to me," he acknowledged. "Instead, she invited me in for coffee and spent the next hour trying to make me feel better."

"Sounds like she's quite a woman."

"She really is," he agreed. "My brother lucked out when he fell in love with Raina. She's been nothing but supportive of his career, despite the fact that she's raising their kids on her own when he's deployed.

"But despite Raina's assurances that no harm had been done, the incident scared the hell out of me. I couldn't risk something like that happening again and really hurting someone, so I decided to leave San Diego for a while, until I got my life back on track.

"Of course, she brought Benjamin to see me before I left. And he apologized to me." Jake shook his head, as if marveling over the fact. "He said he was sorry that he'd cried and he understood I was trying to protect him, because I was a Marine, just like his dad."

He looked away, a muscle in his jaw flexing, and Sky knew he was grappling to maintain control of his emotions.

Just listening to him recount the story had Sky feeling a little teary-eyed herself.

"But I'm nothing like his dad. Luke has done close to a dozen tours in fifteen years, moving steadily up the ranks. He's a gunnery sergeant now, and no doubt he'll probably be a major someday, like our dad."

"Is that what he wants?" she asked.

"It's what we both wanted. Only I couldn't cut it."

She took his hand again, linked their fingers together.

"Obviously I don't know the details of what you saw or did during your time in the Marine Corps, but I think maybe you need to cut yourself a break," she told him. "Everyone's experiences in combat are different, and even those who share the same experiences may process them differently. Anyone can end up with PTSD and it's estimated that between ten and twenty percent of veterans who served in the Middle East do."

"Someone's been doing some research," he noted.

"I spent six years in college," she said. "Old habits are hard to break, but I apologize if I overstepped."

He shook his head. "You didn't."

"So you said that Benjamin's nine, but you'd previously mentioned a three-year-old niece," she said, attempting to maneuver the conversation to a less difficult topic.

"Christina," he said. "And between Ben and Christina is Nate. He's six. Thankfully, he and his little sister were both tucked into bed by the time the kids next door brought out the firecrackers."

"You miss them a lot," she said. "I can hear it in your voice when you talk about them."

"Yeah, I guess I do," he said. "I got to spend a fair bit of time with them over the past couple of years. Kids give you a whole different perspective on life. Maybe it's naïve or idealistic, but they make me believe there's some hope for the future of this screwed-up world."

She nodded, understanding. "I've got two nieces and three nephews, and my sister Kate is expecting another child early in the new year. But I wasn't supposed to say anything about that just yet," she suddenly remembered. "Because they aren't ready for the news to be public knowledge."

"I don't know how I'll resist telling all my friends in town," he remarked dryly.

She smiled then. "You must be feeling better— your smart-ass attitude is back."

"I am feeling better," he said. "Thanks."

But she could see in his eyes the toll that the whole evening had taken on him, so she pushed away from the table and carried their plates to the sink.

"Stop," he said, when she started to run the water.

"What?"

He took the bottle of soap from her hands. "You're not washing the dishes."

"I don't mind."

"I do," he said. "You didn't get the dinner out that you were promised—I am absolutely *not* letting you tidy up the kitchen."

"I used half those dishes," she pointed out.

He picked up the tea towel and dried her hands.

She didn't bother to protest. Instead, she asked, "Do you have any plans for next Thursday night?"

"No."

"I'll bring the pizza then."

"I thought the deal was only valid if tonight went well."

"You didn't have a good time tonight?"

"I had a panic attack in the restaurant."

"Just a little one," she said. "And then we came back here and enjoyed our excellent steaks and loaded baked potatoes."

"I'd say the steaks were more overcooked than excellent."

"Maybe a little, because I reheated them in the microwave," she acknowledged. "But do you know why I said yes when you invited me to go out with you tonight?

"I'll give you a hint," she said, before he had a chance to respond. "It had nothing to do with wine or candlelight."

"Am I supposed to guess now?" he asked.

She shook her head.

"I said yes because I wanted to be with you."

"You really need to set the bar higher," he told her.

"Thursday night," she said again. "I'll bring the pizza."

"Aren't you going to ask what toppings I like?"

"Sausage and peppers," she said, proving that she'd been paying attention when he told her about his second visit to Jo's. Then she brushed her mouth against his. "I'll see you around six."

Chapter Eleven

"Do you really think we're going to eat two pizzas?" Jake asked, when he greeted Sky at the door the following Thursday night.

"Considering that I haven't eaten all day, yes," she told him, reaching down with her free hand to scratch behind Molly's ears. The greeting had the dog's whole back end wagging.

"But if we don't, you can put the leftovers in the freezer," she said, as she toed off her shoes. "Because even reheated, Jo's pizza is better than anything from the frozen foods section in the grocery store."

"Why haven't you eaten all day?" he asked, apparently stuck on that part of her response.

"I was busy."

"Too busy to grab a bite?" His tone was dubious.

"Yeah," she said. "I had a meeting with the guidance department at the high school early this morning about an honor roll student who's suddenly skipping classes and failing tests, then I went to court to provide moral support for a client who was testifying in a custody hearing that will decide whether or not her abusive soon-to-be ex-husband gets unsupervised visitation with their kids. When court broke for lunch, I went back to the high school to talk to the student who was the subject of the morning meeting, scheduled a follow-up with him for tomorrow, then returned to the courthouse for the afternoon session. After the hearing was finally adjourned for the day, I called Jo's to order the pizza, then I picked it up and brought it here."

"And you told me you didn't have a full-time job," he remarked.

"If I did, I'd probably work fewer hours," she acknowledged. Then her gaze snagged on the bottle on the counter. "Is that wine?"

"Yeah. I don't have a clue about grapes or vintages, so I called the restaurant we didn't eat at last week to ask about the reds on their wine list and this one sounded familiar."

"It's one of my favorites," she said, absurdly touched by his effort. "And I would really enjoy a glass of it right now."

"I'll open it," he promised, retrieving a corkscrew from the drawer of utensils. "But I think you should have a slice of pizza first."

"I'm not going to get drunk from one glass of

wine on an empty stomach," she promised, setting the boxes on the table so that she could wash her hands.

"Let's not test that theory," he advised.

"All right." After drying her hands on the towel that hung on the handle of the oven, she reached into the cupboard to retrieve plates for their meal.

"I've got plates in the living room," he said, as he pulled the cork out of the bottle. "I thought we'd eat in there tonight."

"Okay," she agreed, guessing that there was a game that he wanted to watch on the big screen.

She picked up the pizza boxes again and followed him into the living room, stopping short when she saw that he'd draped a cloth over the coffee table and set it with what she guessed had been his aunt's good china, real silver and linen napkins.

She placed the pizza boxes in the center of the table. "What is all this?"

"A feeble attempt to make up for the fact that you didn't get your fancy candlelight dinner the other night. And *damn*—" he finished pouring the wine into her glass, then reached into his pocket for a book of matches "—I forgot to light the candles."

She sipped her pinot noir as he struck a match and held the flame to the wick of the first candle, then the second.

"This is really sweet," she said. "But really not necessary."

He opened the lid of the pizza box and, using an

intricately embossed cake server, lifted a slice of pizza out and set it on her plate.

"Does eating off of good china mean we need to use a knife and fork?" she asked, wondering about the purpose of the cutlery.

"Of course not," he assured her with a shake of his head. "I only put the silverware out because the table setting looked unfinished without it."

"Thank goodness," she said, picking up her slice and biting into it. The flavors of gooey cheese, tangy sauce and spicy sausage exploded on her tongue. "Mmm...*sooo* good."

"And suddenly, I'm feeling unnecessary," Jake remarked dryly.

"Why?" she asked, already bringing the pizza to her mouth again for another bite.

"Because you're making the same sounds over that pizza as you make in the bedroom."

"I am not," she denied.

"Trust me," he said. "I'm intimately familiar with your sighs and moans."

"Well, I've had a very satisfying relationship with Jo's pizza for a lot of years," she told him. "And it looks like Molly wants to get acquainted with it, too."

"No," Jake said to the dog, who was inching ever closer to the coffee table, her nose twitching.

"Do you ever let her have treats from the table?"

"No," he said again, responding to Sky's question this time. "Not only because people food isn't good for dogs but because it gives her gas like you wouldn't believe."

"And how do you know that if you don't give her treats?"

"I learned that lesson the hard way," he admitted. "I used to let her have the occasional piece of cheese or last bite of a burger. And then I realized that those treats had a very specific and undesirable effect."

"Maybe Ashley's been sneaking treats to Rey," she mused. "That little dog makes a really big stink sometimes."

She looked at Molly, who had wriggled close enough that her nose was pressed against Sky's leg.

"Sorry," she said. "But Jake says you're not allowed to have this."

Molly looked at her pleadingly.

"It's not me, it's him," she said, pointing.

The dog actually sighed, making Sky smile.

"How did you two end up together?" she asked Jake now.

"My sister-in-law got her for me from a friend who trains service dogs."

"She's a service dog?"

He chuckled at that. "No. She totally flunked the test to qualify for training."

"And yet, just having a pet can be therapeutic," Sky noted. "Dogs, in particular, can be very intuitive, even without special training."

"She's certainly been good company," Jake said. "And she's always there when I wake up from a nightmare. Sometimes she even manages to wake me, before things get really bad." Then, before she could comment or ask about the nightmares, he continued, "Plus taking her out for exercise ensures that I get exercise, too."

Sky took her cue from him and let the subject of his nightmares drop—for now. "I'm not disciplined enough to exercise every day," she confided.

"It sounds like you spend a lot of time running from job to job every day," he noted.

"That's not the same thing. And between the running today, I spent a lot of hours just sitting on my butt at the courthouse."

"Is that why you're wearing those fancy clothes? Because you were in court today?"

She glanced at her attire, amused by his description. "A jacket and pants are fancy clothes?"

"Comparatively," he said. "Because I'm accustomed to seeing you in jeans and a T-shirt behind the bar at Diggers'. Although the outfit you had on last Thursday was nice, too. And then there was that very memorable day that you were stranded on the roadside wearing a snug little sweater, short skirt and chunky-heeled boots."

"You remember what I was wearing?"

"Oh yeah," he said, nodding. "It was the day I discovered that you've got really spectacular legs."

"Thank you?" she said dubiously.

"Of course, my recollection of what you were wearing under that sweater and skirt is even more vivid." He grinned. "You've got spectacular underwear, too."

"And you haven't even seen what I've got on today," she teased.

"Are you going to let me take those fancy clothes off of you so that I can?"

"I'd be disappointed if you didn't," she told him.

"I won't let you leave here disappointed tonight," he promised.

And proceeded to prove that he was a man of his word.

Jake was hovering in that state of postcoital bliss halfway between asleep and awake when Sky's voice cut through the silence.

"I should be heading home," she said. "It's late."

"Will you be grounded if you miss curfew?"

"I don't have a curfew, but I have a little sister who does and I'm trying to set a good example."

"She does look up to you," he noted.

"How would you know?"

"She talks about you all the time. Or maybe she just talks all the time. Honestly, I sometimes want to tell her to pause and take a breath."

Sky chuckled softly at that, then her expression grew serious. "Do you mind her hanging out here? Does she get in your way?"

"Nah, she's mostly harmless. And Molly loves when she's here, because Ashley will throw the ball forever."

"Rey still prefers to play keep-away," Sky said, sliding to the edge of the mattress to reach for her discarded clothes. "She fetches the ball, but then refuses to let go of it."

"Yeah, we've been working on that a little." He

shifted closer to peer at a blue mark on Sky's skin. "What's this?"

She had to twist her head to see the back of her arm. "Oh. I guess I must have hit the ground harder than I thought."

"Hit the ground?"

She nodded. "When I dove to catch Connor Neal's line drive Tuesday night."

"You got this bruise playing baseball?"

"Making the final out," she clarified. "Which ensured that we won the game."

"Competitive much?" he asked, sounding amused.

"Baseball is more of a passion than a pastime in this town."

"Still, you should be more careful."

"I should be more careful?" she challenged, skimming her fingers gently down his side, over a ridge of puckered skin.

"Yeah, well, that isn't from anything I did on purpose."

"What's it from?"

It was the first time she'd asked. The first time she'd made any reference to his scars, though he knew there was no way she could have missed them when they were naked together.

"I crashed into a market cart…after being thrown through the air when our Humvee was hit by an RPG."

"Afghanistan?" she guessed.

"I did a tour in Afghanistan," he told her. "But that was the last one, in Iraq."

"Is it okay that I asked?" she wondered, sounding worried.

"Yeah. Truthfully, I'm surprised it took you this long."

"I figured if you wanted me to know, you'd tell me. But then…well, you know the thing about the cat and curiosity."

"And now you know," he said.

Which wasn't really true, and he braced himself for the follow-up questions he felt certain would come after his admission.

But Sky surprised him again, only saying, "What I don't know is why you're making a fuss over a little bruise."

"Because I don't like to think about you being hurt."

"It doesn't hurt. Not really. And the bruise will be gone in a few days," she assured him.

"You really dove for a line drive?" he asked, not just to keep the topic focused on her injury rather than his own, but because he really wanted to know.

"I really did," she confirmed.

"I think I'd enjoy watching you play softball," he said.

"Games are at Prospect Park every Tuesday night at seven and the occasional Saturday afternoon at two."

"I'll keep that in mind."

"But I should probably warn you, there isn't a lot in the way of entertainment in this town—"

"Shocking," he said.

"—so we draw pretty big crowds," she continued, pointedly ignoring his interjection.

"What's a pretty big crowd?"

"There are usually thirty to forty spectators at most of our games."

"I'm surprised you don't have law enforcement at the park for crowd control."

"Connor Neal is the deputy sheriff."

"The hitter of the line drive you snagged?"

She nodded.

"You're lucky you didn't get taken in for grand larceny."

"I didn't get a chance to ask you last week about your big date," Natalya said, when Jake showed up at the community center the following Wednesday night.

"I was glad you didn't," he confided. "So that I didn't have to tell you that it was a disaster."

She winced sympathetically. "That bad?"

He nodded and, because it was Nat and he knew she'd understand, briefly summarized what had happened at the restaurant.

"It sounds like Sky handled the situation," she remarked when he'd finished the story.

A lot better than he would have anticipated.

Of course, if he'd anticipated any of it, he would never have asked her to go out with him.

"She did," he agreed. "But she shouldn't have had to."

"Have you seen her since then?"

"Yeah. We had pizza at my place last week."

"And how did that go?" she asked.

"That was good." But it was thinking about what had come after the pizza that made him smile. "Really good."

"So maybe your big date wasn't such a disaster," Nat suggested. "Maybe Sky needed to see your response to a situation like that to know how you'd react—and how she would, too."

"I still don't know that I'm ready for a relationship," he confided.

"Regardless, it looks like you've got one."

"I don't even know how long I'm going to be in Haven."

Nat smiled then. "That's what I said, too—five years ago."

But Jake knew he couldn't stay in Haven.

This was only a temporary detour in his life, and he'd get back on track as soon as he found the track again.

But as he settled in his usual seat for the meeting, he found himself wondering if he was really even looking. And as he listened to others talk, not about the traumas they'd endured but the struggles that came after, he wished that he could do the same.

It wasn't that he didn't want to talk about his experience, but that he couldn't. Every time he thought he was ready to say something, his throat would close up so that he couldn't even speak.

Tonight, after Doug Holland—who'd survived friendly-fire in Syria—finished talking about his ongoing struggle with anger management, Jake decided it was his turn. He was ready to open the gates and let the demons out.

My name is Jake Kelly...

The words were there, but they wouldn't come out.

Apparently he wasn't ready to open the gates after all—or maybe they were rusted shut.

He'd enlisted because he wanted to serve and defend his country. To not just defeat the bad guys but seriously kick their asses and return home a bona fide hero.

By the time Jake was halfway through his first tour, he was no longer concerned about being hailed a hero—he just wanted to make it home alive.

He was proud to wear the uniform. To be a Marine like his dad and his brother. But life in a war zone was a special kind of hell, particularly when the bad guys weren't readily identifiable. The enemy was nowhere and everywhere, and if a man let his guard down for half a second, he could end up dead...

Ask Jonesy, the radio operator who'd gone outside the wire to retrieve an errant football. Except that no one could ask Jonesy anything anymore, because he'd been taken out by sniper fire.

Jake's recon team had a new radio operator now. Corporal Anderson Walker was a third-generation Marine, earning him the nickname Trey. He didn't play football and he sure as hell didn't venture out-

side the wire without a combat helmet and body armor.

But he was a good man.

All the men on his recon team were good men.

Molly nudged his shoulder, waking him before the memory-slash-dream could turn into something darker.

He drew in a deep breath and pushed himself up in bed.

"You want to go for a walk?" he asked.

She waited patiently while he pulled on some clothes.

The night was dark, the sky full of stars, the moon a crescent of silver. The stillness of the countryside had taken some getting used to after living back in San Diego for the past few years. Just as he knew the faster pace of San Diego would take some getting used to after living in Haven for several months.

If he went back to San Diego.

He frowned at that thought.

Of course he was going back. He never intended to stay in Haven permanently—just until he got his life on track, however long that might be.

Later that day, Jake was again in the converted barn, taking inventory of the equipment and supplies and wondering what the heck he was going to do with everything, when Molly barked and left her usual post by the open doors. There weren't many things that drew her from his side, unless they were rabbits, squirrels or Ashley and Rey. So he wasn't surprised when his young neighbor stepped inside the workshop.

"What's going on with you and Sky?" she asked without preamble.

"What makes you think there's anything going on?"

"I'm very intuitive," she said.

"Isn't that just a fancy word for nosey?"

"I've been called that a few times, too," she admitted. "But most people cut me some slack because I didn't have a father for the first twelve years of my life."

"Lots of kids grow up in single-parent homes. How is that an excuse to butt into other people's business?"

"In this case, one of those other people is my sister," Ashley pointed out. "So that kinda makes it my business."

"I don't think Sky would agree with you on that."

"Probably not," the kid acknowledged. "But I can't help but worry about her."

"Why's that?"

"Because she's always so busy taking care of other people that she sometimes forgets to take care of herself."

"Maybe you are intuitive," he noted. "But that doesn't mean you're not nosey."

"I saw her Jeep in your driveway when my mom brought me home from Chloe's the other night."

"And?"

"And then she didn't come home until three o'clock in the morning," Ashley said.

Though he'd teased Sky about having a curfew, he hadn't realized she'd stayed so late—or that she apparently had reason to be concerned about the example she was setting for her sister.

And if he no longer rushed Sky out the door as soon as they finished making love, she seemed to accept that he wasn't yet ready to let her stay overnight. That he wasn't yet ready to let her know all his demons. That his freak out at the restaurant was only the tip of the iceberg.

"But you don't know for certain that she didn't go somewhere else between the time that you saw her Jeep in my driveway and when she got home," Jake pointed out.

"No," she acknowledged. "But she was smiling when she came up the stairs, and she's not usually in a good mood when she comes home after dealing with some kind of crisis."

He was pleased by this confirmation that Sky had left his bed obviously satisfied, but it was the latter part of Ashley's comment that prompted him to ask, "Does she ever talk to you about those crises?"

Ashley immediately shook her head. "She would never violate a client's confidentiality. But I know that Mrs. Morningstar's boyfriend had naked pictures of Jodie because Jodie is Chloe's sister and Chloe's my best friend."

"How old is Jodie?" he wondered.

"Sixteen."

"And she let her mom's boyfriend take naked pictures of her?" His stomach roiled at the thought.

"Oh, no," Ashley was quick to assure him. "She didn't know he'd put a nanny cam in one of her teddy bears."

"I hope he's in prison now."

She nodded. "In Minnesota. He was extra—" She wrinkled her nose, as if thinking hard to remember the word.

"Extradited?" he guessed.

"That's it," she confirmed.

Jake had known that Sky had to deal with some weighty issues as both a youth counselor and volunteer at the women's shelter, but he suspected the situation Ashley was talking about had hit particularly close to home for her because of her sister's connection to the family. Of course, having lived her whole life in Haven, Sky probably dealt with personal connections more often than not.

"So what are you doing in here?" Ashley asked, clearly ready to move on to another topic of conversation.

"Not a whole helluva lot of anything at the moment," he told her.

She made her way around the room, examining the tools and materials.

"Don't touch anything," he cautioned, as she reached toward the miter gauge of a table saw. "I don't want to have to mop up the blood if you chop off a body part."

She immediate snatched her hand away. "Eww."

He held back a smile.

"What is all this stuff?" she asked.

"Mostly tools for making furniture," he told her.

"Is that what you do?"

He shook his head. "No. My uncle was the carpenter."

"I know. He made the table and chairs in our dining room, and the fancy cabinet where my mom keeps her best dishes."

"He made a lot of stuff for other people," Jake said.

Good, quality furniture that would last for generations, and yet a lot of the furnishings in his own home looked like garage sale markdowns. Of course, good furniture cost money, which was in short supply for Ross and Anna Ferguson. So while his uncle had been capable of making heirloom pieces, he couldn't afford to keep them.

"What's this?" Ashley asked, pointing to a tool on one of the workbenches.

"That's a pocket hole jig."

"What does it do?"

"It helps you drill pocket holes so that screws can be inserted at an angle, along the grain of the wood rather than through it. It makes the joint stronger and more stable."

He perched on the edge of a sawhorse, watching as she made her way around the room, pretending to be interested in items whose names and purposes eluded her.

"What are you really doing here, Ashley?" he asked her.

"I'm bored," she admitted.

"Why don't you go hang out at the mall?"

"Haven doesn't have a mall. And I don't have a driver's license, which means I'm stuck out here in the middle of nowhere with nothing to do and no one to talk to."

"Some of us enjoy being in the middle of nowhere *with no one to talk to*," he said, deliberately emphasizing the last part.

She didn't take the hint.

"Maybe you could show me how to make something," she suggested.

"I'm not sure I remember how half these tools work," he told her.

"Oh," she said, sounding disappointed.

"But maybe we could spend some time teaching Rey to drop the ball after she fetches it," he suggested.

The girl immediately brightened. "Okay. But I should warn you, she's not a very quick learner."

More than an hour later, after Ashley and Rey had gone, Jake returned to the workshop and picked up a board from the top of the stack. Though he had forgotten most of what his uncle had taught him so many years before, he had an idea in his mind and nothing else to do at the moment.

Ross had enjoyed working with reclaimed wood. He said the old weathered boards reminded him of himself: one part of his life—his struggles as a cattle rancher—finished and another just beginning. The nicks and scars in the wood were proof of its experience and ensured the finished product would have unique character.

Remembering his uncle's words now, Jake realized that the same analogy could be applied to his own life.

What he'd been, the career he'd had, was no more.

If he wanted to move forward, he needed to reinvent himself.

And maybe he could start right here.

Chapter Twelve

Sky just wanted to go home.

It had been a really crappy day, and now she wanted nothing more than to crawl into bed and pull the covers over her head until morning.

Or maybe next week.

She didn't know what impulse made her turn into Jake's driveway before she reached the Circle G. In fact, she was about to shift into reverse to pull out again when Molly came around from the back of the house, her tail wagging so happily that Sky couldn't bear to disappoint the dog by leaving again without at least saying hi.

So she parked, climbed out of her Jeep and crouched to greet the Lab.

"Hey," Jake said, his lips curving into an easy

smile when he saw her. "I wasn't expecting to see you tonight."

She straightened up, suddenly uncertain again. "Is it okay that I stopped by?"

"Anytime," he replied without hesitation.

Inexplicably, her eyes filled with tears.

"Hey," he said again, tipping her chin up. "What's going on?"

"I just had a really crappy day," she confided.

"You want to talk about it?"

She shook her head. "Could you just—never mind," she decided, already turning back toward her car. "This was a bad idea. I shouldn't have come here. I don't know what I was thinking."

He caught her hand before she could find the handle. "Maybe you were thinking that you needed a friend," he suggested.

"Are we friends, Jake?"

"At the very least," he assured her. "And maybe working toward something more."

She managed a smile, though it wobbled at the edges.

"You want to come in for a cup of coffee?" he invited.

"Yeah, that sounds good, thanks."

Sky sat at the table while Jake moved around the kitchen, filling the reservoir with water, measuring grounds into the filter.

"How about food?" he asked.

"What?"

"Did you have dinner, Sky?"

"Oh." She shook her head. "No."

"I could heat up some leftover pasta for you."

"Thanks, but I'm not hungry."

He retrieved two mugs from the cupboard.

"Want to tell me about your day?"

"I want to, but I can't," she said.

"So what can I do?" he asked.

"Nothing," she said.

"Let's try something anyway," he suggested, tugging on her hands to draw her out of the chair.

She wasn't really in the mood for sex, but maybe that was why she'd come here. Maybe, subconsciously, she'd known that getting naked and sweaty with Jake would push everything else out of her mind—at least for a while.

But instead of starting to unbutton her blouse or even lowering his head to kiss her, he simply put his arms around her and held her close so that she could hear his heart beating, steady and strong, beneath her cheek.

And it was that gesture—the simplicity and sweetness of it—that broke the barrier and the tears that she'd mostly managed to hold in check could be held back no longer. She cried and cried, until there were no tears left, and all the while, Jake continued to hold her.

"I'm sorry," she said, when she finally managed to pull herself together.

"There's no reason to be."

"I soaked your shirt."

He glanced down at the damp fabric. "It needed to be washed anyway."

She tried to smile, but now that the storm of emotion had passed, her head was pounding.

"Do you have any Tylenol?"

"Headache?" he guessed.

She nodded. "I always get one when I cry too much."

"How often is that?"

"Not very," she assured him. "I'm usually pretty good at holding it together, but today was just…" She left the sentence unfinished, but he got the message.

He retrieved a bottle of pills from the cabinet and poured her a glass of water.

"Thanks."

"Why don't you go to my room and lie down?" he suggested, after she'd downed the pills.

The prospect of falling into bed right now was almost too tempting. "Because I should get home."

"You're always looking after everyone else," he said. "Why don't you let someone else take care of you for a little while?"

"You already have," she said. "And I'm grateful."

"You shouldn't get behind the wheel with your head hurting. And you'll feel better after a quick nap."

"Are you sure you don't mind?"

He responded by turning her toward the exit from the kitchen. "Go."

So she went.

Molly followed, then jumped up onto the bed to stretch out beside her.

"I'm going to assume you're allowed up here because I don't want to send you away," Sky said.

The dog settled in, and Sky fell asleep on top of the covers and stayed that way until morning.

Whey Sky woke up, it took her a moment to orient herself to her surroundings and realize where she was.

Jake's bedroom.

She reached over to touch the other pillow, but there was no evidence that he'd been there with her. There were, however, more than a few yellow hairs visible on her pant leg, confirming that Molly had snuggled with her for a while.

She ducked into the bathroom to splash some water on her face, wipe away the smears of mascara under her eyes with a tissue and rinse with the mouthwash on the counter. Then she made her way to the kitchen, where Jake was measuring coffee grounds into a filter.

"Déjà vu," she said.

He hit the button to start the machine brewing, then turned to greet her with a smile. "Good morning."

"When I stopped by last night, I didn't plan to crash," she told him.

"It wasn't a problem."

"Still, you should have woken me up and sent me home."

"I liked watching you sleep in my bed."

"You watched me sleep?"

"Not all night," he assured her. "But I did check on you a few times. Though I needn't have bothered, because Molly stuck pretty close to your side the whole time."

Sky lifted a hand and ruffled the dog's fur, hoping to convey both her affection and appreciation.

"Where did you sleep?" she asked Jake.

"On the sofa."

"That couldn't have been very comfortable," she said, trying to imagine his six-foot frame folded onto a five-foot couch.

His smile was wry. "I've slept in a lot worse places."

"Oh. Right." Afghanistan and Iraq, she remembered now. And possibly other countries that he hadn't mentioned. "In that case, I won't feel too guilty about stealing your bed."

"You shouldn't feel guilty at all. If I didn't want you here, I wouldn't have asked you to stay."

"As I recall, you invited me to stay for a nap."

"And didn't you nap?"

She chuckled. "Sure, we'll go with that."

He set a frying pan on top of the stove and drizzled some oil in it. "I've got bread today, but I'm short on eggs," he told her. "French toast okay?"

"Are you offering to cook for me again?"

"You have to fuel up," he said. "It's a game day and breakfast is supposedly the most important meal."

"It *is* a game day," she said. "But I didn't expect you to remember that."

"I not only remembered, I stopped by the park last week to watch a few innings," he said, as he scrambled the eggs he'd cracked.

"I thought I caught a glimpse of you and Molly by the bleachers at Diamond Two."

"That was us," he confirmed.

"Why didn't you come to the dugout to say hi?"

He shrugged as he dipped a slice of bread into the egg mixture. "You mentioned it was mostly parents or spouses who come out to the games."

"And we don't have that kind of relationship," she said, echoing the words she'd spoken once before. Then she followed up with the question he'd asked her: "So what kind of relationship do we have?"

"I thought we established yesterday that we were friends—and maybe more."

Since he was busy at the stove, she retrieved two mugs from the cupboard and filled them from the coffeepot. "Are you going to come out to the game today?" she asked him.

"I might stop by for a few innings."

"It's a long way into town for just a few innings," she pointed out.

"But totally worth it to see you in those snug-fitting pants," he assured her.

"Maybe I could come over later tonight and you could see me out of them," she suggested.

"Even better."

* * *

Not long after Sky had gone, Ashley and Rey showed up again.

"I didn't expect to see you today," Jake said.

"I wanted to say thanks for texting me last night to let me know that Sky was crashing here."

"I didn't want you to worry—or wait up all night waiting for her to come home."

"I don't know that I would have stayed up *all* night, but I might have worried," she allowed.

"And you did say thanks when you replied to my message," he pointed out.

"I also wanted Rey to get some exercise because she has to be on a leash when we're at the ballpark."

"Right, it's a game day today, isn't it?" he said, as if he didn't already know.

Ashley nodded. "Are you gonna come?"

"Maybe. I've started something in the workshop, so we'll have to see what progress I make."

"I thought you said you weren't a carpenter."

"I'm not. I'm just messing around."

"Are you in the military?" she asked him.

"Not anymore."

"What branch were you in?"

"Marines."

"Once a Marine, always a Marine."

He looked up, both surprised and amused by her response.

"My mom's a big fan of NCIS, and I watch it with her sometimes," she told him.

"I thought kids your age only watched YouTube videos," he remarked.

"I'm not a kid," she said.

"Right. Sorry."

"Why aren't you in the military anymore? Is it because of your PTSD?" she guessed.

"You really do just blurt out whatever's on your mind, don't you?"

She shrugged. "I heard it mentioned when my mom and Sky were talking the other day."

His scowl deepened.

"Sky didn't say that you had PTSD," Ashley hastened to explain. "In fact, she argued that my mom shouldn't speculate about the condition of a man she's never even met, but my mom worries that Sky isn't seeing the situation clearly because of her feelings for you."

"Did you take notes while you were eavesdropping on their conversation?"

"My teachers say I pay close attention to detail."

But Jake could tell it was more than that, and he suspected the girl was worried about the conflict between her mother and half sister. That maybe, despite her outward bravado, she wasn't entirely confident of her place in the world—or even within her new family.

"And I thought you'd be more interested in Sky's response than my listening skills."

"I'm not going to ask what your sister said," he assured her.

Ashley smiled like a cat with a mouthful of feathers. "But you want to know, don't you?"

Yeah, he wanted to know, but he wasn't going to ask—not without knowing for sure that he was prepared to hear the answer.

Prospect Park did double duty as a neighborhood park, complete with swings, seesaws and a climbing structure, and a sports facility, with soccer pitches, baseball diamonds, basketball courts and even a designated area for lawn bowling. In the ballpark area, there were sets of stadium seats behind each of the home and visitor dugouts—if a players' bench behind a length of chain link fence could be called a dugout—and a small concrete-block building with food services at the front and restroom facilities at the back.

The concession offerings were limited to hot dogs, nachos, peanuts, popcorn, candy bars and hot and cold drinks, but there were a handful of picnic tables nearby and several were occupied when Jake arrived.

As he surveyed the scene, he noted that there weren't a lot of empty seats on the bleachers, and most of the spectators proudly displayed their team loyalty with baseball caps or T-shirts that matched the logos of one team or the other. Duke's Diggers wore grey pants with dark blue T-shirts emblazoned with a cartoon depiction of a grizzled prospector holding a pickax in one hand and a gold nugget in the other. The opposing team—the Haven Hawks, sponsored by Jo's—was in red and white.

Jake spotted Ashley, seated in a folding lawn chair behind the backstop, the scorebook in her lap. Rey's leash was tied to the leg of her chair, and the pup was curled up on the grass beside her.

Molly must have spotted them at the same time, because she tensed at his side, eager to take off and visit her friend as soon as he gave her the okay.

Jake didn't give the okay.

"Sorry, girl," he said instead. "Not today."

It was the same thing he'd said to her the last time they were at the park.

And the time before that.

But they stayed until the end of the game today, when the Diggers ran off the field after making the final out, whooping and hollering in celebration of their victory. Sky smiled as one of her teammates tugged on the ponytail threaded through the hole in the back of her hat.

Glad to know that she was having a much better day than the one before, he turned away. "Let's go home, Molly."

Sky glanced around, a seemingly casual survey, as the spectators began to gather up their stadium cushions and concession garbage at the end of the game. She didn't see Jake anywhere, although she'd been certain she'd caught a glimpse of him earlier. And if she was disappointed that he hadn't stuck around, she was pleased to know that he'd been there.

"You had a successful day at the bat," Caleb noted as she packed her bat and glove into her equipment bag.

"Thanks." She tugged on the zipper.

"Two for three with four RBIs," he continued.

"Are you the official league statistician now?" Sky asked.

"Nah. But I was thinking that you've earned yourself a beer," he said. "You coming to Diggers'?"

"Not today."

"Why not?"

"Because I want to get home and shower," she said. "Plus, I promised to drop Ashley off at Chloe's." She had some reservations about her little sister hanging out at Chloe's house since the incident with Leon Franks and learning that Chloe had a taste for vodka coolers, but she understood the importance of the friendship to both girls. More important, she trusted that Ashley had a good head on her shoulders and wouldn't hesitate to reach out if she found herself in a situation that was at all uncomfortable for her.

"No other plans?" he prompted.

"What do you really want to know, Caleb?"

"If there's any truth to the rumors I've heard about you being involved with Ross Ferguson's nephew."

"His name is Jake Kelly," she said. "And since when do you pay any attention to gossip?"

"Since it comes from a trustworthy source."

Sky frowned. "What's your trustworthy source?"

"Our sister."

"Kate?" Sky didn't believe it. There was no way her by-the-book attorney sister would divulge any information that had been shared with her in confidence, even if in the comfort of her own home over coffee and donuts.

Caleb shook his head. "Sorry, I should have said our *little* sister."

"Ashley," she realized.

He nodded. "She said she saw your car in his driveway the other night and then heard you sneaking into the house at three a.m."

"She should have been sleeping at three a.m."

"So it's true?" he asked.

"I'm twenty-five years old," she reminded him. "I don't have to sneak anywhere."

"So it's true," he decided.

"What it is, is none of your business."

"I'm your brother—"

"My brother not my keeper," she interjected.

"I'm worried about you, Sky."

"You don't need to be."

"It's hardly a secret that you have a lousy track record with men," Caleb said, not unkindly.

"No, it's not," she acknowledged. "But thanks for the reminder, anyway."

Her brother sighed. "Come on, Sky. Don't be mad."

"I'm not mad."

"I just don't want to see you get hurt again, and no one really seems to know much about this guy."

"Jake," she said again. "And I know him."

"Do you?" he challenged.

Before Sky could respond to that, Ashley came over to join them. "Are we going to go sometime today? Chloe's texted me five times in the last five minutes."

"We're going right now," Sky promised, shouldering her bag and starting toward the parking lot.

Caleb fell into step beside her. "Just…be careful," he urged.

"I always am." She unlocked the car and Ashley climbed into the back seat with her dog.

"I love you, sis."

And with those words, Sky's irritation melted. Because she knew they were true. She might not appreciate Caleb's interference in her personal life, but she knew that his concern was motivated by affection.

"I love you, too, PITA," she said, using the acronym for *pain in the ass*.

He grinned, relieved to know that he was forgiven.

Sky tossed her bag into the back of her SUV and climbed behind the wheel.

As she drove toward Chloe's house, she couldn't help but reflect on her brother's remarks. Because Caleb was right. She did have a lousy track record with men.

Everyone that she'd loved—or thought she'd been in love with—had left her.

Maybe she shouldn't include Peter Jarrett on that list, because it was probably inevitable that their relationship wouldn't have survived them going to different colleges in different states. But he'd promised her that they'd make it work because he loved her. And she'd wanted to believe him because she loved him, too. Then he'd dumped her before Thanksgiving that first year.

She'd held off falling in love again until her third year at UNLV. But Xavier Leroux had been in his final year, and when he graduated, he moved on to bigger and better things—and another woman.

Archie Collins had been one of her faculty advisors when she was working on her master's thesis—an ill-advised relationship that had probably lasted longer than it should have. But right or wrong, she'd loved him, too. And although technically she'd left him when she moved back to Haven, the end result was the same.

In the end, she was alone.

And she knew that if she fell for Jake, he'd be no different.

He'd already told her that he didn't intend to stay in Haven for the long-term. It was just a temporary stop—a convenient place for him to get his life together.

Staying in this small town had never been part of his future plans.

Except that he didn't really have a plan.

So maybe he would change his mind. Maybe, if he could find the peace here that had so far eluded him everywhere else, he would stay in Haven.

Maybe he'd stay with her.

Chapter Thirteen

Sky didn't make it back to Jake's house later that night.

After driving Ashley to Chloe's house, she took Rey back to the Circle G and left the pup in the care of her father and stepmother so that she could shower off the dirt and grime from the game. She'd just stepped out of the enclosure and wrapped herself in a towel when her cell phone chimed with a text message.

An hour later, Sky was back in town, sitting across from Jenny Taft at the kitchen table in her mother's house.

"I wasn't sure you'd come," the former cheerleader said, sounding both surprised and relieved. "I wasn't very nice the last time I saw you."

"As I recall, you weren't having a very good day."

The other woman managed a smile, then immediately lifted a hand to cover her mouth—and hide the tooth that hadn't been chipped the last time they'd talked.

"So why did you want to see me?" Sky asked.

"When you came to the clinic, you said that there were options…for people in…" She seemed to struggle to say it, to acknowledge the truth.

Sky waited, not wanting to put words in Jenny's mouth.

"Abusive relationships," the other woman finally continued.

"There are always options," Sky assured her.

"He wasn't always…mean," Jenny said. "In the beginning, Darren was really sweet. Even now, sometimes he brings me flowers, or just kisses me softly, and I know he loves me." She dropped her gaze to her hands, folded neatly in her lap. "But those times aren't very often anymore. Not compared to the times that he's mean."

"Can you give me examples of what he does when he's mean?" Sky asked gently.

"He yells. A lot. Almost all the time now." She swallowed. "I know he's unhappy. When we were in high school, he thought for sure he was going to get a football scholarship, but that never came through and he had to go work in the mines, just like his father."

"It's always hard to let go of a dream," Sky acknowledged. "But I bet you had dreams, too, didn't you, Jenny?"

"Not big ones."

"Tell me about them," she urged.

"There was a time that I wanted to be a teacher," she confided. "I always thought it would be nice to have a decent job, go on vacation once a year, maybe to Disneyland with the kids—" her smile was wistful "—after we had kids."

"And now?" Sky prompted.

"Now I know I won't ever have any of those things with Darren."

"Because he yells?"

Jenny nodded. "And sometimes…" She looked at Sky now, her expression stricken. "Sometimes he hits me."

Sky knew the admission wasn't just a crucial first step in moving forward for victims of abuse, but often the hardest one to take. And she credited Jenny's mother for helping her to take that step now.

"I don't want to be hit anymore," Jenny said, her eyes filling with tears.

Sky waited, sensing there was more the other woman wanted to tell her. After another minute, Jenny continued.

"I was pregnant once…about six months ago." She swiped at the tears that spilled onto her cheeks. "I lost the baby. It wasn't Darren's fault—and I'm not making excuses this time. Even the doctor said that sometimes these things just happen."

Sky nodded.

"I cried for a long time afterward. I cried and cried, and Darren got mad at me for mourning a baby that was hardly the size of a pea when I lost it. And I was sad that I'd lost the baby, but I think I was relieved, too. Because I knew that if I had Darren's baby, I'd never get away from him.

"So I went to my doctor and I asked to go back on birth control pills." She wiped away more tears. "The day that you came to see me at the clinic...that was the day he found my pills. He was so mad. I don't think he wanted a baby any more than I did at that point, but he was mad that I'd made a decision about birth control without consulting him."

"What did he do?"

She closed her eyes. "He grabbed me by the hair and shoved me against the wall. He punched me. And he kicked me."

"Are you telling me now that you didn't fall down the stairs that day?" Sky asked.

Jenny shook her head. "I didn't fall down the stairs," she confirmed. "He pushed me."

Though Sky wouldn't have said that she and Jake had settled into any kind of a routine, she was nonetheless surprised when he walked into the bar on Friday night.

"Sam Adams?" she asked, already reaching for a glass.

Jake shook his head. "Give me a shot of Jack Daniels."

Sky set the mug back on the shelf. "Straight up or on the rocks?"

"Straight up."

She reached for a glass and poured a shot of whiskey.

"What's the occasion?" she asked, as she set the drink in front of him.

Jake's only response was to lift the glass to his lips and toss back the alcohol.

"Another one," he said, pushing the empty glass toward her.

Sky frowned but acquiesced to his request. "Are you going to tell me what's going on with you?"

"I'm not here for company or conversation," he said, echoing the words he'd spoken ten weeks earlier.

"That's obvious," she noted dryly. "But I thought we were already friends."

He lifted his gaze to hers then. "You might want to reconsider. Most of my friends don't fare too well."

And there, she knew, was the heart of the story he had yet to tell her. Because the bits and pieces he'd shared about his life before coming to Haven were nothing more than that. But she hadn't pushed, suspecting that if she did, he'd just withdraw further. Instead, she'd waited, confident that he would open up when he was ready.

She hadn't anticipated that he might be ready on a Friday night when she was working in a packed bar. So she poured and mixed, filling orders and keeping an eye on Jake as best she could.

"Another one," he said, nudging the glass toward her again.

She tipped the bottle over the glass. "That's a lot

of whiskey for a guy who usually limits himself to a single draft beer," she remarked.

He tossed back the third shot.

She finished an order for Courtney, then called out to Rowan, who was working the other end of the bar. "Can you hold down the fort for two minutes?"

Her bartending partner nodded as he mixed drinks. "A quick two minutes," he agreed. "That looks like a bachelorette party just coming in."

Sky glanced toward the door and noted the group of women decked out in sparkling tiaras and satin sashes identifying them as bridesmaid, maid of honor or bride.

"I have no doubt you can deflect amorous advances and mix cosmopolitans at the same time," she said lightly.

"Of course, I can," Rowan agreed with a wink. "But your two minutes are ticking."

She ducked away from the bar and into the kitchen, relieved to see that Duke was still there. The owner of Diggers' usually stopped by most nights to check on his business and chat with his customers—and sample whatever was on special from the kitchen that day.

"I'm glad I caught you," Sky said, as her boss carried his empty plate and cutlery to the sink. "I need a favor."

Jake didn't protest when Sky took his arm and guided him through the kitchen and out the back door of the restaurant. In fact, he didn't say anything at all until she opened the passenger door of her Jeep and nudged him in that direction.

"Where are we going?"

"I'm taking you home," she told him.

He shook his head. "I don't want to go home. I want another drink."

She held up the bottle of JD from the bar. "You can have another drink at home."

That seemed to satisfy Jake, as he got into the SUV without further protest.

Molly was, as always, happy to see her master return. And though she let Sky fuss over her, too, she stayed close to Jake's side. The dog might have flunked training, but there was no doubt that she was sensitive to Jake's moods and protective of him.

After walking through the door, Jake immediately went to the cupboard to retrieve two glasses, then reached for the bottle in Sky's hand.

"Don't pour one for me," she said. "Jack Daniels and I broke up a long time ago."

"I don't see much of him anymore, either," he said. "But we still get together once a year."

"Why tonight?"

"Why not?" he countered, and tossed back another mouthful of whiskey.

She moved past him and into the living room, because she sensed it was going to be a long night and preferred not to spend it on a hard chair in the kitchen.

Jake—and, of course, Molly—followed.

He set the bottle and glass on the coffee table before dropping onto the sofa. Frowning, he reached into his back pocket and pulled out his cell phone, then tossed it on the table, too.

"Are you going to tell me what's going on?" she asked.

"Why do you think something's going on? Can't a guy stop by the bar to have a few drinks without an interrogation?" he challenged.

"I'm not interrogating you," she denied, keeping her tone level. "I'm wondering why a man who usually doesn't drink anything more than a single pint of beer when he comes into the bar is suddenly knocking back shots of hard liquor."

Jake knocked back another before replying. "I used to drink a lot. Probably too much and for too long." He stared at the amber liquid in the bottle for a long moment, then shook his head, his expression bleak. "But no amount of alcohol could make me forget."

"How long has it been?" she asked gently.

"Since what?"

"I'm guessing today is the anniversary of whatever happened that led to the end of your military career."

"Not much gets past you, does it?"

"I'm not asking you to share anything you don't want to," she said, ignoring the bitterness in his tone. "I just want you to know that I'm here if you want to share."

"People always want to hear the war stories," he said, pouring another shot. "Like drivers slowing by the scene of a car wreck on the side of the road. There's a morbid fascination…a need to know what went wrong…and a sense of relief that it happened to someone else and not you.

"When they meet someone who's seen action, they want to know all the details of battles fought and won. It's like we're actors playing at war on a movie screen and not real people who wake up every morning wondering if it might be our last.

"And they don't seem to know—or maybe don't care—that most of us don't want to talk about it. Most of us just want all the noise in our heads to go away. Just for a day. Or even an hour." His tone was as anguished as his expression. "And then we feel guilty for wishing that we could forget. Because if we don't remember those who didn't make it back— if *I* don't remember my team—who will?"

"Can you tell me about them?" she asked.

He seemed surprised by her request. "You want me to tell you about my recon team?"

"Actually…can you start by telling me what a recon team is?"

"You don't know much about the military?" he guessed.

"I can give you chapter and verse on breeding cattle, but the divisions and ranks of the armed forces are a mystery to me."

"You learn fast when your boots are on the ground." He poured another drink. "But in answer to your question, Marine Division Recon are the reconnaissance assets of the MAGTAF. Marine Air-

Ground Task Force," he explained in response to her blank look.

She nodded, encouraging him to continue.

"It was our job to observe and report on enemy activity and anything else that might be significant to military operations, such as surveying routes, examining bridges and buildings, assessing LZs and DZs—landing zones and drop zones," he clarified before she could ask.

"How many soldiers are on a team?"

He shook his head. "On a USMC recon team, none. A soldier serves in the army."

"Okay, how many *Marines* are on a USMC recon team?"

"Usually six," he told her. "The team leader, assistant team leader, point man, radio operator, assistant radio operator and slack man."

"You were the team leader?" she guessed.

He saluted sharply. "Staff Sergeant Jake Robert Kelly at your service."

"And the rest of your team?"

"Sergeant Ken Baker was the assistant team leader and one of the toughest guys I've ever known—unless he was talking about his wife or any one of his three daughters, then he was a complete marshmallow. We called him Tex, because he was from El Paso and you could hear hints of his hometown in his voice.

"Our point man was Lance Corporal Calvin Moore, otherwise known as Big Red because he stood six-feet-five-inches tall with a mop of ginger hair. No one was surprised to learn that he'd played on the basketball team in high school, but he'd also played trumpet in the marching band and liked to sing in the shower. Especially AC/DC tunes," Jake said, and smiled a little at the memory.

"Our radio operator was Corporal Anderson Walker. When Tex found out that he was a third generation Marine, he dubbed the RO Trey. Trey was a hardcore video gamer who could kick anyone's ass at *Call of Duty*, but he hated having to fire a real weapon. He didn't hesitate, when the need arose, but he never found any pleasure in it."

It wasn't the names and roles he recited but the personal details that made Sky realize these men had been more than just Marines under Jake's command. They'd been his brothers in arms, his family. And her heart ached for him, because she'd guessed what was coming.

"Corporal Mario Lopez was our ARO," he continued, "nicknamed Merlin because he was nothing less than a wizard when it came to fixing problems with the communications equipment. And there were frequently problems with the communications equipment. He was a quiet guy, totally smitten with his high school sweetheart and counting the days until he could marry her when he got back home.

"And then there was Lance Corporal Brian Lucey, our slack man. He was another one from Texas—San Antonio, I think—but because the name Tex was already taken, he got Ditto. He enlisted as soon as he turned eighteen, desperate to get away from his abusive father. Or maybe he joined the Marine Corps to toughen him up so he could hit back. He had such a chip on his shoulder in the beginning, but he quickly became an integral part of the team."

"How many of them did you lose?" she asked gently.

"Four. Three almost right away, because of their proximity to the blast. Merlin somehow held on for almost seventy-two hours, but he never regained consciousness. Trey was the only other survivor, but he lost the use of both of his legs. I was the lucky one," he said, his tone bleak.

"Merlin recognized Salah-al-din Hajjar walking down the street as we made our way through a remote village near Dohuk. He'd worked with us as an interpreter on an earlier mission and we wanted to get his take on some recent intel, so me and Trey jumped out of the truck to flag him down, just before the RPG hit.

"The force of the blast threw us about twenty feet—or so I was told. I don't remember any of it. And the not knowing is almost as bad…or maybe even worse…than remembering."

She'd seen the ink on his upper arm, of course, and realized it was a list of names:

Sgt Ken Baker.

Cpl Mario Lopez.

LCpl Calvin Moore.

LCpl Brian Lucey.

Now she understood why.

"Theirs are the names tattooed on your arm," she said.

He nodded. "I wasn't there for the funeral. I'd been airlifted back to the US because of the head trauma, and I wanted—needed—in some way, to honor them. To ensure that I don't ever forget—even if I can't remember what happened.

"The doctors say it's not unusual after a brain injury, but I can't help thinking that if I could only remember, there might have been something I could have done …something that might have ensured they all came home."

"You can't hold yourself responsible for what happened," she told him.

"But I am responsible. It was *my* team. They were *my* men." He scrubbed his hands over his face to wipe away the tears that had spilled onto his cheeks. "Tex had a wife and three kids. Merlin was planning to get married. They were good men. They didn't deserve to die. And there was no reason for me to live, except that I jumped out of the truck to try to catch up with Hajjar."

She knew there were no words that could possibly make him feel any better. Sure, she could tell him that it wasn't his fault, but no doubt he'd already been told the same thing by countless people before her. It didn't matter that it was probably even true. The only thing that mattered was the grief and the guilt that obviously weighed heavy in his heart.

"We want to believe that we'd more easily accept the tragic events that happen if only we could understand why," she said. "As if there could possibly be some reason or higher purpose that would help it all make sense. But even if that were true, it doesn't really change anything. Knowing the how or why certainly can't bring back the lives of those we've lost."

He nodded and lifted his glass to his lips, then put it down again to look at her more closely. "Who did you lose?"

"My mom," she confided.

"How?"

"She died in a riding accident when I was seven. I'm not trying to equate her death with the loss of your men," she hastened to assure him. "I only wanted you to know that I understand how the what-ifs can haunt you."

"You were seven—what could you have done any differently?" he wondered.

"Had oatmeal for breakfast."

He looked at the nearly empty bottle of JD. "Either I've had too much of this or not enough, because that didn't make any sense to me."

"My mom loved to ride," Sky explained. "Every morning after we'd all had breakfast, she'd saddle up Honey and go for a ride.

"The morning of the accident, I overslept a little, and everyone else had finished eating by the time I sat at the table. She had a bowl of oatmeal waiting for me, but I wanted toast with Grandma's homemade strawberry jam."

"Make your own stupid toast," Katelyn had said.

Because Mom had invited Katelyn to go riding

*with her that morning, and Sky's sister was eager
to get started.*

"I want Mom to make it," she'd insisted.

"Maybe if I hadn't insisted on having toast that
morning, my mom would have started out on her
ride five minutes earlier. And maybe when she got
to the ridge, whatever spooked her horse wouldn't
have been there yet and she wouldn't have fallen.
She wouldn't have died."

And Kate wouldn't have had to watch it all unfold.

"It's hard not to wonder," Jake acknowledged.

She nodded, because she knew Kate still wondered, too. If she'd called 9-1-1 using their mom's
cell phone instead of riding back to the house for
help, could the paramedics have got there in time
to save her?

Jake offered his glass to Sky. "Are you sure you
don't want some of this?"

"I'm sure," she said, taking the now-empty bottle
from his other hand.

He'd undoubtedly overindulged and would pay
the price tomorrow, but he hadn't drunk as much as
he probably thought because the bottle she'd brought
from the bar had been more than half empty before
she'd even poured his first shot at Diggers'. She returned from the kitchen, only a couple of minutes
later, with a glass of water and the bottle of Tylenol
to find Jake asleep on the sofa.

Sky didn't worry about trying to get him to the
bedroom. As he'd pointed out to her once before, he'd
slept in worse places than the sofa in his living room.

She did worry about the nightmares he'd mentioned and the likelihood that they would plague him tonight. But as reluctant as she was to leave him alone to battle those demons, she sensed that he wouldn't want her to stay. Maybe they were gradually working their way toward a real relationship, and maybe they'd taken a few steps closer tonight, but they weren't quite there yet.

So she put the glass and the pills on the end table, plugged his phone into the charging cable there, and gave the Lab a scratch behind her ears.

"Take care of him, Molly."

The dog lifted her head, as if to acknowledge the request, but she didn't move from Jake's side.

So Sky pulled a blanket up over both of them and headed back to her own home. Once there, she sat outside on the porch steps for a while, leaning against a support post to look up at the stars and pray to the heavens that her wounded warrior would find peace.

Chapter Fourteen

Jake felt the press of something cold and wet against his cheek. "Go away," he muttered.

Molly nudged him again.

He sighed wearily. "I really need to put in a doggy door."

And while that was probably a good plan for the future, the idea was absolutely no help to him now.

Molly whined.

He pushed himself into a seated position and opened bleary eyes just as his phone began to blast *Reveille*—the ringtone he'd assigned to his brother's number. It had seemed funny at the time. This morning, not so much.

He grabbed for the phone—not because he wanted to talk to Luke so much as he wanted the damn music to stop.

"'Lo," he said, wondering if the hoarse syllable was his own voice. His mouth felt as if it was stuffed with cotton, his head felt as if jackhammers were trying to break through his skull and his whole body ached.

"Jake?"

He cleared his throat. "Yeah."

He kicked off the blanket that was tangled around his legs and rose to his feet. Molly raced to the door.

"I've been going out of my mind with worry. Why didn't you return my calls?"

"You called?" He opened the door, squinting against the bright morning sun as the dog streaked past him.

"I left four, maybe five, voicemail messages yesterday," Luke said impatiently.

"I didn't get any—oh." As the fog that surrounded his brain began to clear, memories of the night before slowly came into focus. "The battery on my cell phone died when I was out."

"You sound like hell," his brother said bluntly. "Are you drunk?"

"Nah." He measured kibble into Molly's bowl, wincing as even the sound of the dry food dropping into the metal container hurt his head. "Just hung over."

His brother let out a heavy sigh. "I should have been with you yesterday. You shouldn't have been alone."

"I don't need a babysitter. And… I wasn't alone," he admitted.

"Getting up close and personal with Jack Daniels doesn't really count as having company."

"Ha ha," he said. But then, because he understood that his brother was sincerely worried, he added, "A real live person was with me last night, along with JD."

"Have you been making friends out there in the middle of Nowhere, Nevada?"

"I've gotten to know some people," he said vaguely, opening the door again to let Molly in. She raced over to her bowl, skidded to a stop and plopped her butt down, waiting for his signal.

He gestured a wave and she immediately dug in.

"Well, that's good then," Luke said, though his tone was dubious. "Any idea when you're coming home?"

"No."

"Benjamin's been asking about you."

"Me or Molly?"

The dog lifted her head up momentarily, then resumed eating.

"Well, the two of you are a package deal," Luke said.

Jake managed a chuckle. "Tell him I'll bring her for a visit soon."

"It's Dad's birthday next month. Why don't you come home then?"

"Because the last family get-together didn't end so well," he reminded his brother.

"That wasn't your fault," Luke said.

"No one else freaked out over the sound of fire-crackers."

"Maybe you just have faster reflexes than me and Dad."

"Yeah, that's it," Jake said dryly.

"Well, if you don't have any plans to come home in the near future, maybe I'll come out to see you," his brother suggested.

"That's really not necessary, Luke."

"I know it's not necessary, but I want to come."

"Why?" Jake asked, equal parts curious and wary.

"Because you're my brother and I haven't seen you in a long while."

"I'm fine," he said.

"You don't sound fine."

"I overindulged a little last night," Jake acknowledged. "It's something I do once a year."

"It's been three years."

"I know how long it's been," he snapped back.

"Of course, you do," Luke agreed. "I'm sorry."

He sighed. "No, I'm sorry. I'm hungover and short-tempered."

"How about the weekend after next?" his brother suggested.

"Would it matter if I said no?"

"Not likely."

After he'd disconnected the call, Jake wandered back to the living room and dropped down onto the sofa.

He noticed the glass of water on the side table then, and a bottle of Tylenol beside it.

Sky, of course. Always taking care of other people.

He wrestled with the childproof cap, swallowed a couple of pills, then stumbled to the kitchen again to put on a pot of coffee.

While the coffee was brewing, he let the hot water of the shower pound on his shoulders as memories of the previous evening slowly came together in his mind.

Mostly he remembered Sky. She'd been there and taken care of him. He'd bared his soul to her, sharing all of his deepest and darkest secrets. And he'd cried. And while she hadn't run screaming into the night, he had to wonder if—in the light of day—it would prove to be too much for her.

After he was showered and dressed and starting to feel at least a little bit better, he carried his cell phone with him into the kitchen. She hadn't called or texted yet, but he didn't want to miss it when she did.

If she did.

Molly was dancing by the door when he opened the cupboard for a mug to pour his first desperately needed cup of coffee. "You already went outside and I'm going to need a couple more hours and gallons of coffee before I even think about going for a *R-U-N*," he said, just as a soft knock sounded.

"You were telling me that we had company," he realized, as he opened the door to Sky.

"Did I knock too loudly?" she asked in lieu of a more traditional greeting. "I didn't want to make too much noise, in case your head was hurting this morning."

He stepped back to allow her entry. "In case?"

She winced in sympathy. "How bad's the hang-over?"

"I've had worse."

"Maybe this will help." She handed him a travel mug.

"I've got coffee on in the kitchen."

"It's not coffee," she said. "It's the tried-and-true Gilmore secret hangover cure."

He looked wary. "What's in it?"

"It's a *secret* hangover cure," she said again.

He looked dubious as he lifted the lid to examine and sniff the contents. "It doesn't smell too bad," he allowed.

"Try it," she urged.

He took a tentative sip, then another.

She set a grocery bag on the counter, then picked up the mug of coffee he'd poured and lifted it to her lips.

"That was my coffee," he said.

"Coffee's a diuretic and you need to hydrate," she pointed out.

"Still taking care of me, huh?"

"Hangover Basics One-Oh-One."

"Thanks. And for everything you did last night, too."

"I didn't really do anything," she denied.

"You were here for me."

"I didn't want you to be alone. And the fact that you came into Diggers' instead of buying a bottle and bringing it back here suggested to me that you didn't really want to be alone, either," she said.

"I don't keep alcohol in the house," he confided, as she began to unpack the grocery bag. "What's all that?"

"I wasn't sure what you had in your fridge, so I brought a few things over to make breakfast—unless you've eaten already."

He shook his head and eyed the ingredients: eggs, ham, ricotta, red pepper, spinach.

"Are you going to make omelets?"

"A frittata."

He narrowed his gaze. "Isn't that just another word for quiche?"

"No, a quiche has a crust." She set a pan on the stove and began prepping the ingredients. "You don't have to give up your 'real man' card today."

"Didn't I forfeit that last night?"

"No." She met and held his gaze. "Real men aren't afraid to show emotion."

"Speaking of," he said, though it wasn't a very smooth segue, "my brother called this morning. He's planning to come to Haven for a visit."

"You don't sound happy about that," she noted.

"I'd be happy to see him if he didn't have an agenda," Jake told her.

"What's his agenda?" she asked curiously.

"To check up on me."

"That's not an agenda—it's the job of big brothers," she said, as she dumped the spinach and peppers into the pan. "When is he coming?"

"The weekend after next, apparently." He finished the secret hangover cure and grabbed another mug from the cupboard.

"Two more glasses of water before coffee."

"Anyone ever tell you that you're bossy?"

"All the time," she said unapologetically.

He reached for a glass and filled it with water. "*Anyway*, I was wondering if I could ask a favor."

"Of course," she replied without hesitation.

"Would you…when Luke is here…would you…pretend to be my girlfriend?"

Pretend?

It required a concerted effort for Sky to keep the smile on her face so that Jake wouldn't know how much his offhand request had both disappointed and hurt her. Because although they hadn't defined their relationship—beyond a vague "friends…and maybe working toward something more"—she'd started to think that hanging out and having off-the-charts sex together meant that she actually *was* his girlfriend, no pretending required.

Obviously that was her mistake.

She poured the egg-and-cheese mixture into the pan. "Why do you think you need a pretend girlfriend?"

"So he'll stop worrying that I'm isolated and alone in the middle of Nowhere, Nevada."

"He's your brother—why can't you just tell him the truth?"

"And what do you think the truth is?" Jake wondered.

"That you're making progress toward getting your life back on track," she said.

"Is that really how you see it?" he asked her.

"Of course it is. And I would think, if anyone could understand what you've been through, it would be your brother, who's spent fifteen years in the military," she pointed out.

"That's exactly why I can't tell him," he said.

"I don't understand," she admitted.

"Luke is doing what we were both supposed to do—but he's a success and… I'm a failure."

She immediately shook her head. "You're not a failure. You're a hero."

He scoffed at the notion. "My brother has a wife and three kids, and I'm afraid to even let you spend the night in my bed."

"You're just afraid that I'll steal the covers," she teased.

He managed a smile at that, but it quickly faded. "I'm broken, Sky."

"That happens sometimes when people have to endure too much," she acknowledged. "And then sometimes they need some help putting the pieces back together."

"What if the pieces won't fit back together?" he wondered aloud.

"They might not fit in quite the same way, but they're all part of the whole. Although, if you're really concerned, you might want to look into something more focused than a once-a-week meeting at the community center," she ventured. "There are residential PTSD treatment programs available at private facilities in Nevada and California and lots of other places."

"You've been doing research again," he guessed.

"I'm trying to help."

"I already told you how you can help when Luke comes to town."

Despite the pang of disappointment in her heart, she couldn't refuse his request—or resist the opportunity. "Okay, I'll pretend to be your girlfriend when your brother comes to visit *if* you agree to be my date for my brother's wedding next weekend." She made the offer hopeful that the outing would help Jake realize that though he'd always carry the scars of his former life, he'd already started to make a new one in Haven—with her.

"How many brothers do you have?" he asked.

"Two."

"Aren't they both married already?"

"They are," she confirmed. "But Caleb and Brielle eloped in Vegas eight years ago, with no one there to celebrate with them, so they're having a belated reception next Saturday."

He hesitated.

"I promise I won't leave your side for a single minute."

"You know I'm not good with crowds," he said. "I barely managed to stay at the bar the night the baseball team was there."

"But since then, you've actually been out to watch some of the games."

He didn't sit on the bleachers, with the other spectators, but she knew that his willingness to even venture into the park was a step in the right direction.

"That's just because I like the way you look in the uniform," he told her.

"Apparently you like the way I look in short skirts, too," she reminded him.

"Will you be wearing a short skirt to this wedding?"

"Is your willingness to accept the invitation contingent on the length of my hem?"

"Maybe." He grinned. "I do like your legs."

"And I did buy a new dress for the occasion when I was shopping with Ashley the other day, and the skirt falls to about here—" She touched her thigh, a couple of inches above her knee.

"Then my answer is yes," he said. "I just hope you don't regret asking."

"How much longer are we gonna be stuck in this godforsaken dust bowl?" Tex asked.

"Nine weeks and six days," Merlin told him.

"But who's counting?" Jake asked dryly.

"Merlin's counting the days to his wedding." Ditto followed up the remark by humming a few bars of Mendelssohn's Wedding March—*horribly off-key.*

"More like his funeral," Big Red said.

Because ribbing one another was how they passed the time, and joking about death helped lighten the mood when they were living and working in hostile territory.

Jake tuned them out, mostly, and let his thoughts drift.

Nine weeks and six days.

That didn't seem so long now. Not after almost ten months had already passed.

He could understand why Merlin was eager to get home and celebrate with a wedding. They missed so much when they were gone. Not just important dates and special occasions, but everyday stuff, too.

Maybe he'd talk to Margot about setting a date for their wedding. They'd been together for less than six months before his first deployment, but even then he'd known that he wanted to spend his life with her. So when she'd hinted that a ring on her finger would reassure her that he loved her as much as she loved him, he hadn't hesitated to put one there.

She'd been happy enough with the ring that she hadn't pressed him to set a date. The subject did come up every once in a while, but their timelines were always vague... "sometime in the next couple of years" or "maybe next summer."

He knew he was lucky to have her. It wasn't easy for a woman to stick with a man who could be gone for months at a time, maybe even longer, and she always seemed happy enough to talk to him when he was able to call. She didn't nag at him or get all weepy like he'd heard other guys grumble that their girlfriends, fiancées, wives or lovers did. Margot was always proud and supportive, thrilled to be able to tell everyone she met that her fiancé was a Marine.

Maybe it was time to change that status to hus-

band and start the rest of their lives together, Jake mused.

Maybe—

He was flying through the air even before he heard the boom of the explosion.

Did his life flash in front of his eyes?

He didn't think so, though there had been flashes of moments and memories as he seemed to fall in slow motion—right up until he slammed into the ground.

He woke up in a cold sweat, trembling from head to toe, his hip throbbing, his ribs burning. He scrubbed a hand down his side to reassure himself there was nothing broken, no blood spilling onto the packed earth.

"Deep breaths. In and out through your mouth."

He wasn't on the ground. He was in his bed.

He wasn't in Iraq. He was in Haven, Nevada.

"Let the air fill your chest...hold it there...then slowly let it out again."

Molly pressed closer to his side, her chin propped on his chest, her presence calming him as nothing else could.

He lifted a shaky hand to stroke it down her back.

"Deep breaths. In and out through your mouth."

He closed his eyes and concentrated on his breathing, though he knew he wouldn't get any more sleep that night.

Another Wednesday. Another meeting.

Tonight Bill Seward was telling the group about

his most recent communication with Lan Nguyen, a woman he'd known back in Vietnam and with whom he'd recently reconnected through social media. She'd invited him to come for a visit and Bill was intrigued by the idea of seeing her again, but he wasn't sure he was ready to face all the memories that a return to the country would inevitably dredge up.

The group wasn't much help. Some were encouraging him to take the trip, to take a chance, others were cautioning him against making any hasty decisions, and a few—like Jake—were keeping their thoughts and opinions to themselves.

"Let us know what you decide to do," Nat said, ready to move on.

"I will," Bill promised.

"Anyone else want to share anything?" she asked, her gaze moving around the circle.

Jake was sweating through his shirt, but his throat was as dry as the desert. He shifted in his chair, the movement causing one of the metal legs to scrape against the floor.

Nat looked at him, silently encouraging.

"My name is Jake Kelly," he began, then had to pause to clear his throat. "I was a staff sergeant in the Marine Corps before I was sent home with my brain scrambled...

He didn't talk for very long. He wasn't ready to tell this group of not-quite-strangers his deepest and darkest secrets, but it was a start. An important start, he acknowledged to himself. And hopefully the beginning of some real healing.

When the meeting was finally over, he was more than ready to head to Diggers' for a drink—and to see Sky.

"Jake—"

He paused at the door when Nat called out to him.

"—can you hang on for just a sec?"

"Sure," he agreed, remaining where he was until she'd finished chatting with Geena Perrault.

"Do you need a ride home?" he asked when the other woman had gone, guessing that was why Nat had asked him to wait.

"Thanks, but Kevin's coming to get me." She glanced at her watch. "Very soon, in fact, so I'll make this quick."

He held out his hand, palm open and facing up.

She lifted a brow.

"I'm not going to get a gold star for speaking up in class tonight?"

"If I'm not mistaken, you already got a purple heart."

He narrowed his gaze. "How is it that you know things people don't tell you?"

"Because I know other people," she said. "And I ask the right questions."

"Well, since you apparently don't need a ride and I'm not getting a star, what did you want to talk to me about?"

"A partnership opportunity."

"I'm listening," he said, more wary than curious.

"I have a friend, Connie, who trains emotional support animals in Indiana—at least, she has for the past twelve years," Nat explained. "But now she and her husband are moving to Battle Mountain, so she's looking for a place to board and train the animals locally as well as someone to help her out. Since you have a fair amount of space at your ranch and time on your hands, I thought of you."

His immediate instinct was to say no without any questions asked, because a partnership sounded too much like a commitment and Jake wasn't ready to make a commitment to anyone or anything. But while he'd been telling himself that Haven was merely a detour on the map of his life, he'd been struggling for months—years—to find his own path again. And now he had to wonder...could this be it?

"I appreciate the thought," he said instead, perhaps a little surprised to realize it was true. "But I still don't know how long I'm going to stay in Haven."

"That's what you keep saying," she acknowledged. "In any event, you don't have to be here to rent your barn and yard to Connie."

"I'll think about it."

"But if you decide to stay," Nat continued, "you might actually enjoy working with her."

"Training dogs?" he said dubiously.

"You've done a decent job with Molly."

"Molly failed her training as a service dog. Actually, she didn't even get that far. She failed the test to get into training."

"The standards for service animals are much higher, the requirements much stricter," she pointed out. "Emotional support animals are companions that provide support and comfort."

Exactly what Molly did for him.

And the more he thought about it, the more intrigued he was by the idea of helping others in similar situations find pets that could help them.

"When is your friend moving to Nevada?"

"Not until September. But she's going to be in Battle Mountain next weekend, house hunting with her husband, if you want to meet her."

"I'll think about it," he said again.

Nat's smile was just a little bit smug. "I know you will."

Chapter Fifteen

"Is this First Date, Take Two or Second Date, Take One?" Jake wondered aloud, as he tucked his shirt into his pants.

Molly didn't even lift her head off her paws, a sure sign that she was pouting. Obviously she'd figured out that he had plans for the evening that didn't include her.

"I'm leaning toward Second Date, Take One," he said. "And leaving the disaster that was First Date on the cutting room floor."

He turned away from the mirror to face the dog. "Stop sulking." But he did feel a little guilty that he was abandoning her to another night home alone. "You'll always be my best girl, but Sky looks much better in a dress."

Molly was unmoved by his platitudes.

"And maybe, if I don't freak out during Second Date, Take One, then Sky will come back here later. You'd like Sky to come for a visit, wouldn't you?"

That got a half-hearted tail wag.

Jake scratched behind her ears. "I'll try not to be too late," he promised.

Molly still didn't seem happy, but she rose to her feet and followed him to the door.

Tonight, Jake was picking Sky up at the Circle G. If she had any residual concerns about him meeting her family, she'd pretty much tossed them out the window by inviting him to be her date for a family wedding.

He pulled up close to the house and got out of his truck, inexplicably nervous. Sky opened the door before he could knock. Obviously she'd been watching for him, probably because she wasn't convinced that he'd actually show up. Truthfully, he'd had some moments of doubt himself, but not only was he there, he was on time and—

Wow!

Jake didn't know much about women's fashions, but he knew what looked good—and Sky looked *really good*.

She was wearing a halter dress made of some kind of flowy material in a deep blue color that brought out the blue in her eyes. The strappy silver sandals on her feet added several inches to her height, so that her mouth—shiny with pink gloss—was almost level with his. Her hair was up—no doubt in deference to the heat—and glittery blue stones dangled from her ears.

"You told me about the length of the skirt," he acknowledged. "But you didn't warn me that my heart would go into palpitations when I saw you wearing it."

"Then I guess it's lucky for you that I know CPR," she told him.

"Maybe you could start with some mouth-to-mouth," he suggested.

"Like this?" she said, and brushed her lips lightly over his.

"That's a good start," he agreed, drawing her into his embrace.

His hand skimmed upward, over the silky fabric—and even silkier skin bared by the low back of her dress—to cup her head, adjusting the angle and deepening the kiss. Her lips parted willingly, her tongue dancing and dallying with his. Her scent, something soft and floral, teased his nostrils and clouded his mind.

"I think your heart is just fine," Sky said, when she'd finally pulled back and taken a moment to draw air into her lungs. "And if we don't get going, we're going to be late."

"You really want to go to this thing?" he asked, more resigned than enthused about their plans.

"Considering that 'this thing' is my brother's wedding, yeah," she said. "Plus, we had a deal."

"I know," he admitted. "But now that I see you in that dress, I really want to get you out of it."

She brushed another quick kiss on his lips. "Later."

He knew that word was as good as a promise.

Because even after five weeks, the passion between them had yet to dim. He wasn't convinced that it could last, and he was certain there would come a time when really great sex wouldn't be enough, when she would want more. And Jake wasn't sure that he was capable of giving her any more—no matter how much he might want to.

He pushed those uneasy thoughts aside for now and turned his truck in the direction of the Silver Star. "Is it true that Caleb and Brielle split up shortly after their wedding, eight years ago, because your grandfather had a heart attack when he found out?"

"Not my grandfather, Brielle's grandfather—who's also Ashley's grandfather," she noted.

"That's right. She told me that part of the story," he remembered. "So is the grandfather going to be there today?"

"Not only will he be there, he's hosting and paying for the whole thing," Sky told him.

"Really?"

She nodded. "I think he feels guilty for driving a wedge between them all those years ago and this is his way of trying to make up for it." She gestured to a laneway ahead. "That's the Silver Star."

Jake put his indicator on and made the turn into the long drive.

He understood that this formal reception acknowledging the marriage of Brielle Channing and

Caleb Gilmore was a big deal because of the acrimonious history between the families. He hadn't realized that it was going to be such a big event. Based on the quantity of vehicles that lined either side of the laneway and the number of people milling about, he would guess that half the town was in attendance.

Sky must have been taken aback by the size of the gathering, too, because she said, "We don't have to stay all night."

He nodded. And while he appreciated her willingness to accommodate his limitations, this was something he wanted to do for her. Because it was important to her and she was important to him.

As they made their way through the crowd, Jake was surprised to realize that he'd already been introduced to a fair number of the guests in attendance.

Sky's sister, Katelyn, was actually the first person he'd met in town, as her office had been his first stop to get the keys to his uncle's house when he arrived. He hadn't known then that the attorney was married to the sheriff, or that they had a daughter—the little girl who'd shown him her starfish pose at the community center.

Liam was the next oldest, after Kate. Sky had mentioned that Liam and his wife Macy had three kids. She hadn't mentioned that they were triplets. As if chasing after three toddlers didn't keep the couple busy enough, he learned that Macy also managed the day-to-day operations of the Stagecoach Inn while

Liam helped his father and brother keep everything running smoothly at the Circle G.

After Liam was Sky, then Caleb. He'd been the youngest of Dave Gilmore's offspring for a long time, until they'd discovered that Valerie Blake's daughter, Ashley, was their half sister.

In addition to her siblings and their spouses and kids, Jake was introduced to Sky's father and stepmother, her grandparents and various aunts, uncles and cousins, some having come from fair distances to share in the celebration.

"I can't believe how completely they managed to transform a horse paddock into the perfect venue for a wedding reception," Sky remarked to him.

As it was his first visit to the Silver Star, Jake couldn't remark on the transformation, but he had to admit the setting was nice. Everywhere he looked, there were buckets overflowing with greenery and white blooms. Fence rails had been draped with evergreen boughs decorated with more white flowers and bows. Bistro lights were strung overhead to illuminate the temporary dance floor when it got dark, and nearby was the food tent, reputed to contain long tables with an abundance of hot and cold foods, layered trays of sweets and cookies, a champagne fountain, kegs of beer and coolers filled with sodas and juice pouches.

But before Jake and Sky could get close enough to check it out, they were cut off by Ashley.

"Hurry," she urged, directing them toward rows

of chairs set up facing a gazebo. "The ceremony's about to start."

"Ceremony?" Sky echoed.

Her sister rolled her eyes. "This is a wedding, you know."

The bride wore a floor-length vintage lace wedding dress with cap sleeves, a wreath of flowers on her head and cowboy boots on her feet. Her groom was in a Western tux complete with cowboy hat and boots. And as Brielle Channing and Caleb Gilmore renewed their vows in front of their families and friends—including their infant son, Colton, who watched from the arms of his maternal great-grandfather—there was no doubt that love had finally triumphed over the feud between their families.

"I'm sorry," Sky whispered. "I really thought this was just supposed to be a party in celebration of their marriage, not an actual exchange of vows."

"I'm not freaking out," Jake assured her. "Well, not because your brother and his bride are making promises about forever, anyway."

Sky linked their fingers together and squeezed his hand. "Everyone will spread out after the ceremony. Well, they'll make a beeline for the food, and then they'll spread out."

They were part of that beeline when the *I do*'s were finally done. After they'd filled their plates, they found an empty table tucked in the corner, but their solitude didn't last for long.

Liam wanted to dance with his wife, so he dumped

the triplets on "Auntie 'ky"—as Jake had heard Tessa call her. Thankfully, Ashley came over to help with Ava, Max and Sam, followed by Kate and Tessa, then Regan Neal, sister of the bride and wife of the deputy sheriff, joined them, adding two more babies— her twin daughters, Piper and Poppy—to the mix.

Jake pushed his chair back from the table, ostensibly to make room for the newcomers but also to give himself room to breathe.

"Everything okay?" Sky asked, perhaps concerned that he was going to bolt.

He nodded. "I'm just going to check out the desserts."

"Oh, you have to try the brownies," Regan told him.

"And the cheesecake bites," Kate said.

"Can you bring me a pineapple square?" Sky asked hopefully.

"If there are any left," Ashley said. "Grandma's pineapple squares never last long."

"I'll do my best," Jake promised, and made his escape.

Of course, checking out the desserts had been an excuse to get away from the table, but now that he had a mission, he was determined to track down a pineapple square for Sky.

Looking around the gathering, he had to wonder why she'd invited him to come. She certainly didn't need him there to keep her company, surrounded as she was by family.

And kids.

There were a lot of kids running around.

A lot of babies being cuddled and kissed.

Watching her with her nieces and nephews, it was readily apparent that they adored her as much as she adored them.

It was equally obvious to Jake that she was the type of woman who was meant to have a family of her own.

The idea shouldn't have made his chest feel tight. He didn't have to worry that she had expectations of a future or a family with him. They both knew that whatever this thing was between them, it was only temporary.

Except that it didn't feel temporary when he was with her.

Dalton Butler, another regular at the Wednesday night veterans' group, had talked about the difficulties of going home after being deployed, the challenges of trying to fit into a life that no longer fit him after everything he'd seen and done.

Jake could relate to what he'd said. He'd felt the same way in San Diego.

But here it was different. In Haven, he felt as if he could start again with a clean slate.

And when he was with Sky, there was nowhere else that he wanted to be.

Sky was alone with Colton when Jake finally returned, not just with one pineapple square but a whole plate of them.

"They were restocking the tray when I got there," he told her.

"And since everyone else is gone, I don't have to share," she said, gleefully reaching toward the plate.

"How about sharing with the guy who battled back hordes of salivating wedding guests to bring them to you?" he suggested.

"I guess I could share with him," she agreed, holding a square close to his mouth.

He bit into the pastry, his lips closing around her fingertips, suckling on them gently.

"Don't you go getting me all stirred up when I'm sitting here with a baby in my arms," she said.

He grinned, unrepentant. "Do you stir up so easily?"

"All you have to do is look at me," she confided.

"I want to do more than look—I want to dance with you."

"Really?"

"Really."

"In that case, let's polish off our dessert, find another babysitter for Colton and hit the dance floor."

Valerie scooped Colton out of her arms before Sky could even ask if her stepmother wanted to look after the baby for a while. Sky knew that her father's wife had been disappointed that she'd only ever had one child of her own—and she was overjoyed that her marriage to David Gilmore had given her lots of grandchildren to love and spoil.

While Sky was talking to her dad and his wife,

she noticed that Jake was in conversation with Reid by the bar. On her way to meet up with her date, she stopped to chat briefly with her cousin Haylee, visiting from California, and when she turned around again, she saw that her date had been waylaid by the groom. With a shrug, she headed for the bar to get a glass of wine—and have a little chat with her brother-in-law, who was standing on the periphery of the crowd, sipping his beer.

"I saw you talking to Jake a little while ago," she noted. "What was that about?"

"I wasn't giving your date a hard time," he promised. "I just wanted to let him know that we'd arrested the motorcyclists who'd been racing on the highway."

"You were able to identify them?"

"Thanks to Jake."

"What did he have to do with it?" she asked curiously.

"He's the one who gave us a description of the drivers, their bikes and partial plate numbers."

Obviously he was more observant than she, because Sky had only seen a blur when she'd been pressed up against Jake's truck. Or maybe it was the presence of the man that had made it difficult for her to focus on anything else.

"That's good then," Sky remarked.

"What isn't good is that you didn't tell me about your close encounter with the reckless trio," Reid said.

"I didn't see the point when there was nothing I could add. Everything happened so fast."

"Regardless, I don't want you to ever hold out on me again," he admonished sternly.

"Or what?" she couldn't resist challenging.

Her brother-in-law didn't hesitate to bring out the big guns. "Or I'll tell your sister."

"No more holding out," she promised.

"One more thing," he began.

She eyed him warily over the rim of her glass as she sipped her wine. "What's that?"

"She likes him."

"Who likes whom?"

"Katelyn likes Jake," he clarified. "And she's generally a good judge of character."

Sky smiled then and kissed her brother-in-law's cheek. "Good to know, because I like him, too."

"I didn't think I was ever going to get you alone," Jake said, as he moved with Sky on the dance floor.

"You haven't had a horrible time tonight, have you?"

"It hasn't been horrible at all," he assured her.

"Good."

"But this part is definitely my favorite. I like the way you feel in my arms."

She tipped her head back to smile at him. "That's convenient, because I like being in your arms."

"Of course, naked in my arms would be even better."

"Hold on to that thought for just a little while longer."

"I've been holding onto it all night. It's the only reason I'm still here."

"I know this isn't easy for you," she said. "And I hope you know that I'm grateful you agreed to come with me today."

"I'm not sure your father approves of me being here."

"Did he say something to you?"

"No words are needed when I can see him glowering from clear across the paddock."

"That's not personal," she assured him, as the last bars of the song they'd been dancing to faded into the night.

The tempo of the music immediately changed, and the dance floor was suddenly packed with bodies twisting and gyrating.

Jake backed away from the crowd and closed his eyes.

"Let the air fill your chest..."

"Jake?"

"...hold it there..."

Sky slid her hand down his arm, uncurled his fingers to link them with her own.

"...then slowly let it out again."

"Are you okay?"

He managed to nod.

He was okay, it was just a lot of noise and a lot of people.

But he needed to get out of here.

There was too much noise.

Too many people.

He needed to be alone.

Sky squeezed his hand gently, reminding him of her presence.

And when he looked at her, everything and everyone else faded away, making him realize that he didn't really want to be alone—he wanted to be alone *with her*.

"Are you ready to go?" she asked.

He nodded. "I'm sorry, I just—"

She lifted her free hand and touched her fingers to his lips, silencing his explanation. "I'm ready to go, too."

Sky didn't worry about saying goodbye, even to the bride and groom. After all, they were celebrating the beginning of their happily-ever-after and she was still looking for hers.

Was she foolish to think that she might find it with Jake? To believe that he might finally be the man who could love her enough to want to stay with her?

She knew it was too soon to be making declarations or dreaming of a future for them, especially when he wasn't even ready to call her his girlfriend. But she felt as if they'd made definite progress tonight.

And the night wasn't close to being done.

Of course, they first had to spend some time fussing over Molly when they got back to his place. But Sky didn't mind one bit. Over the past several weeks, she'd fallen in love with the dog right along with the man.

Too soon, she reminded herself sternly.

When they finally made it to his bedroom, Sky unhooked the fastening of her halter and wiggled out of the dress so that she was standing in front of him wearing only a teeny tiny bra and even tinier panties in matching ice-blue lace.

"I'm having those heart palpitations again," he warned.

"You better lie down—" she pushed him back, so that he fell on top of the bed "—and let me take care of you."

He shifted up on the mattress and she straddled his hips with her knees.

"Did I ever tell you how glad I was that you ran out of gas that day?"

She chuckled as she unfastened the buttons that ran down the front of his shirt. "You think I ended up in your bed because you played Good Samaritan?"

"That role seemed to appeal to you more than that of sullen stranger," he noted.

"You only think so," she told him, opening his shirt to run her hands over the rippling muscles of his chest and stomach. "The truth is, the first time that sullen stranger walked into Diggers', I knew that I wanted him."

"The first time?" he said skeptically.

She nodded. "Oh, yeah. The moment our eyes locked, my heart started to pound inside my chest and I thought, he's the one who will finally end my extended period of celibacy."

"When I saw you, I thought, 'This woman is going to be trouble.'"

She paused with her hand on his belt. "You said something along those lines before you kissed me the first time," she recalled.

"What I didn't know then was that you'd be worth every minute of it."

"As long as you know it now," she said, and lowered her head to kiss him.

He let her be in control for about two minutes, then he flipped her onto her back, quickly discarded the rest of his clothes and lowered himself over her.

Now *he* kissed *her*, and it was long and slow and deep. Then he skimmed his mouth over her jaw… down her throat…and lower to nuzzle the hollow between her breasts.

His shadowed jaw rasped against her tender flesh, making her shiver. Then his lips found her nipple, and the shocking contrast of his hot mouth on her cool skin made her gasp, made her yearn.

As his mouth continued to taste and tease her breasts, his thumbs hooked the sides of her panties, tugging them over her hips and down her legs. He nudged her thighs apart and his thumbs glided over the slick flesh at her core, parting the folds, seeking and finding the center of her feminine pleasure.

She was quivering with want, with need, when he finally reached for the square packet on the bedside table to sheath himself before burying himself deep inside her.

From the beginning, there had been passion between them. But now, in addition to that passion, there was tenderness and affection. He held her hands above her head, their fingers entwined, as their bodies moved together in a sensual rhythm as old as time, pushing them ever closer to the pinnacle of pleasure—and over the edge. And he captured her mouth again as he found his release.

If she'd been thinking clearly—if she'd been able to think *at all*—she wouldn't have said it. She would have clenched her jaw tight and pressed her lips together to hold back the words. But her brain was pleasantly fuzzy in the aftermath of passion and her heart was so full that the words just slipped out, a whisper against his lips: "I love you, Jake."

The words filled Jake with equal parts joy and terror.

And while he couldn't deny that he'd developed strong feelings for Sky during the time that they'd been together, he was still reluctant to trust that what they had together was real. Afraid that he would somehow end up hurting her without ever intending to. And even more afraid that Sky might wake up one morning and discover that he wasn't really what she wanted or needed—and that he never would be.

So he didn't respond to her announcement except to ask, "Will you stay with me tonight?"

Chapter Sixteen

Sky hadn't expected a reciprocal declaration. Well, maybe there was a tiny part of her that had *hoped* Jake might have come to the realization over the past five weeks that he was in love with her, too. But she understood that he was wary of getting involved and his heart was still healing. Not just from the loss of the men who had been like brothers to him—although that scar was undoubtedly the deepest, but also the abandonment by his fiancée and the lack of support from his father, who she thought should have been his staunchest ally.

But his family was his to figure out. She just hoped he knew that she had his back. Wherever. Whenever.

And maybe he did know, because when he awoke in the night, sweaty and shaking, he reached for her.

Of course, he had to reach over Molly, who'd jumped up onto the mattress as soon as Jake started muttering and thrashing. Sky didn't object to the Lab's presence because she knew Molly was looking out for her master, and the dog retreated to her own bed again as soon as she knew he was okay.

And then Sky used her hands and lips and body to show him the truth and depth of the feelings in her heart.

When Jake awoke in the morning with Sky in his arms, he had the strangest sensation inside his chest. A sense of belonging, as if he was exactly where he needed to be. That with Sky, he hadn't just found home but peace.

Except that it was crazy to be planning a future with a woman just because he'd managed to sleep through the night with her in his bed.

I love you, Jake.

The words she'd whispered to him echoed in his head, tempting him with possibilities and promises.

But he'd heard those words before.

He'd even let himself believe them.

Sky wasn't Margot—he knew that. And he couldn't help but wonder how things might be different now if he'd met her first. If he'd known her before his life had fallen apart.

She wouldn't have stopped loving him.

He knew her well enough now to be certain of

that. Sky was smart and strong, sexy and fun, loving and compassionate and fiercely loyal.

She was everything any man could ever want in a woman.

But he wasn't worthy of her love.

Not now.

Maybe not ever.

Jake was already up and cooking breakfast when Sky made her way to the kitchen.

"I could get used to waking up to this," she said.

Right away, she realized her mistake.

The stiff smile that curved Jake's lips turned into something that more closely resembled a grimace before he turned away to fill a mug with coffee for her.

"Thanks," she said.

He nodded.

"You look like you were out running already this morning," she said, searching for a neutral topic of conversation.

"Yeah. Now that the warmer weather's here, it gets too hot for Molly later in the day," he said. "And we're usually up early, anyway." He gestured toward the table with the spatula in his hand. "Have a seat. This is just about ready."

She sat, and he put a plate of sausages and eggs in front of her.

"So is it confirmed that your brother's coming to town next weekend?" she asked, as she picked up her fork and poked at her eggs.

Jake nodded as he settled across from her.

"I'm scheduled to talk to the seventh and eighth graders about online safety at the elementary school on Friday, but other than that, I'm available whenever you want me to meet him."

"Actually, I've been thinking about what you said, and I've decided that you're probably right."

"Words I always like to hear," she said lightly. "But maybe you could be a little more specific."

"I should be honest with Luke."

She nodded slowly. "I did say that."

"And you were right. It's past time to stop pretending and own up to what my life really is."

"Your life is nothing to be ashamed of, Jake."

"It's nothing to be particularly proud of, either."

"I guess we'll have to agree to disagree about that," she said. "Because I truly believe you should be proud of not just who you are and what you've done in the past, but everything you're doing now."

"I'm not really doing anything now."

"No? Because it looks to me like your uncle's workshop is undergoing another transformation."

"A friend of Nat's is looking for a place to board and train emotional support animals," he acknowledged. "I'm just trying to see if the space would be suitable for her needs."

"Oh," she said, feeling not just deflated but annoyed with herself for getting her hopes up.

Jake cut off a bite of sausage and popped it into his mouth.

Sky pushed her eggs around some more. "So…

when am I going to get to meet your brother?" she finally asked.

"I don't know what Luke's plans are for his visit. We might not be able to coordinate schedules."

"Now I get it," she said. "This sudden urge to be honest with him is a way of cutting me right out of the picture."

He didn't even deny it. "I'm trying to do what's best for you, Sky. And if we keep doing this…if we continue spending time together…"

"Spending time together?" she echoed, stunned. "Is that all this has been to you?"

"You have to know that I care about you, but—"

"I *love* you, Jake. Maybe I didn't intend to let those words slip out last night, but I'm not sorry they did. I'm tired of trying to deny what's in my heart and hiding the truth of my feelings so I don't scare you away."

"I *am* scared," he admitted. "Mostly of the possibility that I'll end up hurting you."

"Newsflash, Jake—if you didn't want to hurt me, you wouldn't be dumping me without giving our relationship a real chance."

"I'd only end up hurting you more if I tried to be the man you want and need."

"You *are* the man I want and need," she insisted.

He shook his head. "I told you from the beginning that I was a bad bet."

"I didn't believe it then and I don't believe it now," she said.

But it was obvious to Sky that *he* believed it, and she knew that no one but Jake could change that.

She pushed her chair away from the table and carried her plate to the sink.

"Please, Sky…"

"What?" she demanded, when he faltered. "Please, Sky, *what*?"

He only shook his head.

Molly, sensing the tension between her two favorite people, whined plaintively.

The sound squeezed Sky's already bruised heart.

"That's the problem," she said. "You don't know what you want. Or maybe you do know but you're afraid to admit it. Afraid to take a chance on everything I'm offering."

She slid her feet into her sandals and grabbed her purse.

"When you figure it out, you know where to find me."

Sky hated being a fool.

But it wasn't the first time and, considering her track record with men, it probably wouldn't be the last. And while it sucked that she couldn't seem to make a romantic relationship succeed, she had a good life. She had her friends and her family and work that she enjoyed—and maybe it was time to reconnect with some of those friends.

Alyssa Channing was first on the list. They'd chatted briefly at the wedding about rescheduling

their aborted lunch from several weeks back, but
now they actually did so.

"It's so good to finally be able to sit down and
catch up with you," Alyssa said, after the waitress
had delivered their meals to the table the following
Saturday afternoon.

"It's been a crazy busy summer."

And so much had happened since the last time she
was here with Alyssa—the same day that she'd run
out of gas on her way home after meeting with Jodie.
The same day Jake had come to her rescue and she'd
ended up back at his house. In his bed.

Had it only been six weeks?

Had she really fallen in love so quickly?

"Tell me all about it," Alyssa urged. "And don't
spare any of the sexy details about your military
man."

"Actually, that's old news," she said. "I'm not seeing Jake anymore."

Her friend winced. "I'm sorry."

Sky waved a hand dismissively. "Let's not waste
our time talking about it."

"Your call," Alyssa assured her. "But I should
warn you that he just walked into the restaurant."

Of course, Sky had to look.

And as her gaze met Jake's across the room, she
silently berated herself for not considering the possibility that their paths might cross this weekend.
Jake didn't venture into town very often, but she
should have expected that he'd take his brother out
for a meal while Luke was in town. And since din-

ing options in Haven were limited, she should have anticipated that they'd end up at Diggers'.

"Do you want me to ask Geena for takeout containers?" Alyssa said. "It's a nice day for a picnic in the park."

Sky shook her head. "No, this is good," she lied. "But it is a nice day, so we could take Lucy to the park for a walk after lunch."

"And maybe stop at Scoops for ice cream on the way?" her friend suggested hopefully.

"Definitely."

And if Sheila Enbridge, the proprietor, wanted to speculate that Sky Gilmore was soothing her broken heart with three scoops of chocolate fudge brownie supreme, she really didn't care.

Jake couldn't finish his lunch and get out of Diggers' fast enough.

The whole time he was eating food he didn't remember ordering and couldn't taste, he cursed himself for not foreseeing that he might run into Sky at the restaurant where she worked.

True, she worked on the bar side and she hadn't actually been working, but he should have anticipated the possibility.

If you realize you've let your guard down, it's already too late.

"For someone who's been here almost five months, you haven't really made yourself at home," Luke remarked when they were back at the house.

"Why do you say that?"

His brother gestured to the kitchen walls. "If this was my place, those flowers would have been the first thing to go."

"I thought about it," Jake said. "But I wasn't sure how long I was going to stay and I didn't want to start any major renovation projects that I wasn't going to stick around to finish."

"And now?" Luke asked.

He shrugged. "I'm still not sure how long I'm going to stay."

He only wished he had somewhere else to go.

Somewhere he wouldn't be assailed by thoughts and memories of Sky every way he turned.

"Well, at least Uncle Ross finally updated some of the furnishings." Luke ran a hand over the smooth wood surface of the kitchen table. "He did really good work, didn't he?"

"Actually, I made that table," Jake told him.

His brother's brows lifted. "Guess you were paying attention when he was showing us how to use all those fancy tools."

"I didn't remember much," Jake said. "The table's a pretty basic design."

"Basic or not, it looks great." Luke put both palms flat on the top and pushed forward and back, then grinned at his brother. "Just checking to see if it's level."

"Might be that both the table and the floor aren't," Jake said.

His brother chuckled. "I'm going to be honest, when Mom first told me that you were going to be staying here awhile, I didn't think it was a good idea. But maybe I was wrong. Maybe this is the right place for you right now."

"I thought maybe it was, too. But now I'm not so sure."

"Your doubts have anything to do with the attractive brunette you kept stealing glances at during lunch?" his brother guessed.

"Yeah," he admitted.

"So why didn't you introduce me to her?"

"Because I screwed up—just like I always do."

"I would have liked to meet her, but not making an introduction is hardly a screwup."

"No, I meant that I *screwed up*," he said again, with emphasis this time.

Understanding flashed across his brother's expression. "Ah. Now I get it. But maybe you could fill in some details for me?"

Jake shook his head. "You're only here for a couple of days, and it would take longer than that to explain."

"So buy her some flowers and tell her you're sorry," Luke suggested.

"Does that work with Raina?" he wondered.

"Sometimes," his brother said.

"What do you do the other times?"

Luke grinned. "R-rated stuff in the bedroom."

Jake winced. "TMI."

"You asked."

"My mistake."

"So start with flowers," his brother urged.

"She deserves someone better than me."

"I'm probably a little biased," Luke admitted. "But I don't know anyone better than you."

"A former Marine with PTSD and no career prospects?"

"A decorated veteran who's steering his life in a new direction."

"That's a good spin," Jake acknowledged.

"I don't know how I'd cope if I didn't have Raina and the kids to go home to, and I've never had to deal with anything as up close and personal as you did," his brother said. "What happened to your team would have messed up anyone, and sometimes even having family to ground you isn't enough."

Then Luke slid a business card across the table.

"What's this?" Jake asked.

"It's the number for a residential treatment facility specializing in PTSD."

"You've been asking around for help for your crazy brother?"

"No." Luke held his gaze. "I asked my therapist if she knew of any good programs in this area."

Jake frowned at that. "Since when do you have a therapist?"

"Since about six years ago," Luke said.

"For real?"

His brother nodded.

"How did I not know this?"

"Because it's not the type of thing we talk about."

Jake wasn't sure if the "we" was intended to refer

to their family or veterans, but he could acknowledge that both interpretations were equally applicable.

"It was Raina's idea," Luke told him now. "When I came back from my third—or maybe it was my fourth—deployment, she suggested that talking to someone about my experiences might help me transition back to civilian life."

"Did it?"

His brother shrugged. "It doesn't hurt."

"Six years?" Jake looked at his brother again for confirmation. *"Really?"*

Luke nodded. "I talk to her about once a month, if I'm in town. More often if necessary. And Raina and I go together a couple times a year."

"Why didn't you ever tell me?"

"Because I didn't want you to know. I didn't want anyone to know. But I've realized that pretending everything is okay doesn't make it so, and healing is an ongoing process.

"No one expects that a thirty-day program is going to miraculously stop the nightmares and flashbacks or make you let go of your guilt and grief. But it just might help you learn to live with it and move on with your own life. Maybe even with the brunette from the restaurant."

Jake shook his head, refusing to be tempted by the prospect. "She deserves someone who doesn't have to deal with that kind of stuff."

"Maybe she does," Luke agreed. "But from where I was sitting, I'd guess the woman wants *you*."

* * *

Jake's brother left Haven on Sunday.

Sky was aware of his departure because she saw his truck in Jake's driveway when she drove past on her way to the Trading Post just after lunch, but it was gone when she returned home a short while later.

Jake's truck had been missing, too, though she'd let herself believe he was only running an errand. But when she passed his house again the following day, she realized he was gone—and she suspected that he wasn't coming back.

It wasn't just that the driveway was empty, it was that his house looked closed up. Abandoned. Lonely.

That was kind of how she felt, too.

"Why do I always put my faith in the wrong people?" Sky asked her sister, over coffee and donuts the following Sunday morning.

"Are we talking about any wrong people in particular?" Kate asked.

She nodded. "Jake Kelly."

Her sister seemed surprised. "Watching the two of you together at Caleb and Brielle's wedding reception, it looked like things were going well."

"I thought so, too," Sky said.

"What happened?"

"I don't know." Then she sighed. "Or maybe I do know."

"If you want me to commiserate and empathize, I'm going to need a little more information than that," Kate said.

"We had a great time that night. Actually, we had a lot of great times over the past few weeks, but now…" she blinked back the tears that stung her eyes "…now he's gone."

"Where'd he go?"

Sky shook her head. "I don't know."

"He didn't tell you?"

"He didn't even say goodbye."

Her sister responded to that with a single word that questioned Jake's parentage.

"Ba-turd," Tessa echoed.

Kate winced. "Oh, that one's going to come back to bite me."

"Ba-turd," the little girl said again, confirming her mother's prediction.

"Come here, Tessa." Sky patted her knee.

Her niece climbed up and immediately reached for the cell phone Sky had pulled out of her pocket. She pointed to the screen.

"This is bat turd," she said, enunciating carefully. "In some places, it's used as a fertilizer to make flowers grow pretty."

"I 'ike fwowers."

"Do you think you could maybe draw me a picture of a flower?"

"O-kay," Tessa said, scrambling down from her aunt's knee to search for her crayons.

"You are a marvel," her sister said to Sky. "And he obviously has no idea what he walked away from."

"I feel so lost, Kate. Lost and sad and confused and so many other emotions. All those times I cried over broken relationships… I don't think my heart has ever really been broken before. Not like this."

"Maybe because you were never all the way in love before," Kate suggested.

"What does it say about me that when I finally did fall, I picked a guy who couldn't love me back?"

"I wouldn't be so sure that he doesn't love you."

"He left," she said again. "Without a word."

"And for that he's flower fertilizer," her sister agreed, making Sky smile through her tears. "But without knowing why he left, you can't claim to know what's in his heart."

"That doesn't make me feel any better."

"I don't know if there's anything that will," Kate admitted. "And I can't think of anything to say that doesn't sound patronizing or cliché."

"Give me something," Sky pleaded.

"It will get better," her sister said. "Each day, it will be a little bit easier to get out of bed, to go on with your life without him."

"I know I can live without him," Sky said. "I just wish he'd given me the chance to show him how much better both our lives could be together."

"Do you want me to have Reid track him down and arrest him?"

"On what grounds?"

"Breaking and entering your heart?" Kate suggested.

Sky managed another smile. "A tempting thought, but no. Right now, I think the only thing worse than living with a broken heart would be for Jake to know that he broke my heart."

"Are you sure he's gone for good?"

"I'm not sure of anything," she admitted. "All I know is, one day he was here, the next day he was gone."

"And maybe tomorrow he'll be back."

But Sky wasn't going to let herself count on it.

"How are you doing?" Sky asked when she met Jenny at the courthouse the following Thursday morning.

"I'm scared," the other woman said. "Not of Darren as much as everything else that's going to happen."

"That's understandable," she said. "But I'm going to be here with you. If you have any questions about anything, ask."

"I feel like such an idiot."

"You're not an idiot," Sky said firmly.

"But I let him do it for so long… Do you think the judge will believe I liked being hit?"

"No, I don't think the possibility will even cross the judge's mind."

"He—Darren—" Jenny clarified "—said that if I ever told, people would think that I liked it."

"He only said that because he didn't want you to tell," Sky reminded her.

Jenny nodded. "I wish I had a lawyer. I know you said I should get one, but Darren closed out all the accounts, so I have no money. My parents offered to help, but they don't have a lot of money, either, and they're already doing so much for me."

"You do have a lawyer," Sky said, watching her sister walk into the courtroom. "In fact, here she is now."

Jenny followed the direction of Sky's gaze, but she still looked confused when the introductions were made.

"I appreciate you being here," she said to Kate. "But I can't afford a lawyer."

"I'm taking your case pro bono," the attorney said. "That means you don't have to pay for my legal services."

"But why would you do that?" Jenny wondered.

"I have a full-service practice with a lot of clients who can pay, and that allows me to help other clients who can't."

"I don't know how to thank you," Jenny said. Then her gaze shifted to Sky. "Either of you."

"There is one thing you can do for me," Sky said.

"What's that?"

"Go back to school and get that teaching certificate you always wanted."

"You don't think I'm too old?" Jenny asked, half skeptical and half hopeful.

"It's never too late to follow your dreams," Sky told her.

"That's good advice," Kate said, looking at her sister. "For all of us."

Chapter Seventeen

"Get your head in the game, Gilmore."

Caleb's sharp rebuke snapped Sky back to the present.

"What?"

Her brother shook his head. "You're on deck."

"Oh." She swapped her baseball cap for a batting helmet and jumped up from the bench to head toward the on-deck circle, grabbing her favorite bat on the way. She took her position and gave a practice swing.

Joel Rosenthal hit a line drive straight into the second baseman's mitt for the third out of the inning.

Sky leaned her bat against the fence and caught the glove that her brother tossed to her. She traded the batting helmet for her ball cap again and jogged out to her usual position on third base.

"Head in the game," Caleb reminded her, as he moved past her to left field.

She pushed her preoccupation aside and focused her attention on the batter stepping up to the plate.

A walk-off two-run homer resulted in a 5–4 loss for Diggers' in their second game of the round-robin tournament leading up to the Heritage Day Slo-Pitch Charity Championship. It was their first loss—and not Sky's fault in any way—but she knew that, depending on the scores of the other games, it might be enough to jeopardize their appearance in the championship.

"Everything okay with you?" Caleb asked as they were packing up after the game.

"Sure," she replied, not looking at him. "Why do you ask?"

"You seemed a little distracted tonight."

"I've just got a lot on my mind."

"Anything you want to talk about?"

She shook her head.

"Work stuff?" he guessed.

It was a believable excuse—and certainly easier than acknowledging the truth—so she nodded. Because she didn't want to admit to her brother, or even herself, that she couldn't stop thinking about Jake. Wondering where he was and what he was doing. Because it was pathetic to want a man who didn't want her, and the fact that he'd left town was a pretty clear indication that Jake didn't want her.

She impulsively hugged her brother.

"What was that for?" Caleb asked warily.

"For being you."

"The most amazing brother in the world, you mean?"

"And because I'm grateful to know that you'll always be in my corner, no matter what."

"Always," he confirmed.

The championship game of the Heritage Day Slo-Pitch Charity Championship was at three o'clock the following Saturday afternoon. Despite their earlier loss in the round-robin, Duke's Diggers advanced to the final against Sweet Caroline's Sweethearts—a group that was anything but a bunch of cream puffs.

It seemed to Sky as if the whole town had turned out to watch the big game, packed onto the bleachers or huddled along the sidelines in folding lawn chairs, their feet propped up on coolers.

The Gilmores were out en masse. Katelyn and Reid and Tessa; Liam and Macy with Ava, Max and Sam; Caleb's wife Brielle with baby Colton; her dad and Valerie; and Sky's grandparents. Duke was there, too, not only to cheer on his team but add coaching assistance at third base. In addition, she recognized several of the bar's regular customers: librarian Lara Reashore, theater owner Thomas Mann, and even Jo had entrusted her staff to watch over the pizza ovens so that she could take in at least part of the game.

It was a closely contested event—at least in the beginning. But the Diggers rallied for six runs in the bottom of the sixth, which put them ahead by five. And yet, Sky couldn't help but notice that Ashley didn't seem as excited by the prospect of victory as everyone else on their side of the diamond. Even when they held onto the lead until the final out, the scorekeeper's cheers were uncharacteristically subdued.

After the players had shaken hands and the championship trophy was presented, the field quickly emptied of players and spectators.

"What's wrong?" Sky asked, when most of her teammates had gone, leaving her alone in the dugout with her sister.

Ashley shook her head. "Nothing."

"I thought we had a deal, that you wouldn't say nothing when it's obviously something."

"It's my own fault, for expecting too much of people," her sister said unhappily.

"Anyone in particular?" Sky pressed.

Ashley started to shake her head again, then stopped. "Yes," she admitted. "But I don't want to talk about him."

"Ah," Sky said. "This is about a boy."

"No," her sister immediately denied. "Well, yes. But it's not who you think."

"We're not talking about Chloe's boyfriend's friend, the one you met at the movies?"

"No. It's… Jake."

"Jake?"

Her sister nodded. "I texted to tell him about the game today. I thought maybe he'd had enough time to realize how much he missed you and he'd come to watch and then you'd get back together."

Sky had to swallow around the lump that had risen in her throat. "Oh, Ashley."

"He didn't even reply to my message."

"I'm sorry."

"Why are *you* sorry? You didn't do anything wrong."

"I'm not sure Jake did anything wrong, either."

"How can you say that?" her sister demanded. "He left without even saying goodbye."

To Ashley, too, Sky realized now.

"I can say that because I know he's dealing with a lot of stuff right now—stuff that no one should have to deal with," she said gently.

"It doesn't matter," Ashley decided, but her tone told Sky that it mattered a lot.

"Okay," she agreed. "Just remember that I'm here if you ever want to talk."

"I know," her sister said. And then, more hesitantly, she added, "I'm here for you, too, if you ever want to talk. I know you probably think I'm just a kid, but I'm a pretty good listener."

"You are a pretty good listener," Sky said. "And a really great sister."

Ashley smiled at that.

Sky put her arm around her sister's shoulders. "Come on," she said. "Let's go celebrate our victory with a root beer."

The championship trophy was three feet of polished plastic, as gaudy as it was tall, but it came with bragging rights—at least until the season ended, when a new champion might potentially be crowned. The victors passed it around with the same reverence afforded the World Series trophy, and after all the players had had the opportunity for a photo with the Champions Cup, Duke took it back to the bar to put on display.

"What do you think?" the boss asked, as he pushed the liquor bottles on the top shelf to the sides, making space in the middle for the award.

"It looks good," Sky said approvingly from the other side of the counter. She glanced questioningly at Ashley, who nodded as she sipped her root beer.

"It sure looks a helluva lot better than you do," her boss remarked.

Sky lifted a hand to her swollen cheek. "Those leg guards that catchers wear are hard."

"We were up by five runs at that point," Duke pointed out as he wrapped some ice in a towel. "Why you felt the need to slide head-first into home plate instead of staying put on third—*like I told you*—is a mystery to me."

"I was safe at home," she reminded him.

"Yeah, you were safe," he grudgingly acknowledged, handing the towel across the bar to her.

She applied the ice to her cheek as Geena set two plates of burgers and fries in front of them. "Thanks."

"Are you girls going back to the park for the fireworks later?" Geena asked as Sky nibbled on a fry.

She shook her head. "After this, I'm going home to soak my weary muscles in the hot tub."

"But it's Heritage Day," Geena reminded them.

"A time to celebrate with friends and family and py-rotechnics in the sky."

Sky appreciated the sentiment, but she didn't re-ally feel up to celebrating—especially when the one person she'd planned to *not* celebrate with was gone.

Each day, it will be a little bit easier, Katelyn had promised.

And, after three weeks, Sky was finally starting to think it might be true.

She still missed Jake. Every morning when she woke up, he was the first thought on her mind, and every night when she went to bed, he was the last. Wherever he was, she hoped he was doing okay, and that Molly was close by, watching over him.

It figured that just when Sky had finally stopped hoping Jake would walk through the door, he did so.

More than five weeks after he'd left town, on a Wednesday night at just about 9:55 p.m., he came into Diggers', took his usual seat at the bar and—casually, as if nothing had ever happened between them and he hadn't been gone for more than a month—ordered a draft beer.

Not a Sam Adams, though.

This time, he asked for a pint of Icky.

There were so many emotions warring inside her that Sky didn't know what she was feeling. Joy. Anger. Relief. Frustration. Love.

Taking her cue from him, Sky went through the motions, as if she was pouring a beer for any other customer on any other night. As if she hadn't given him her heart—and had her offering summarily rejected.

She shut off the tap and set the mug of beer on a paper coaster in front of him, pleased to note that her hands were steady though her insides were shaking like leaves in a hurricane-force gale. She had so many questions, about where he'd been—and about why he'd come back—but she didn't let herself ask them. She didn't let herself give him any hint of how much she'd missed him, though there was no denying that she had.

Jake didn't say anything, either, but he looked at her over the rim of the mug as he lifted it to his lips, and his gaze held hers for an endlessly long moment. She wished she could read his expression, but she'd never been able to guess what he was thinking and she didn't dare let herself speculate.

But she kept an eye on him while she continued to serve and chat with other customers at the bar. She didn't want to look away, for fear that if she let him out of her sight for a second, he'd disappear again.

Wherever he'd been and whatever he'd been doing for the past five weeks, he looked good. Really good.

Almost as if he'd been on vacation.

And maybe he had.

Maybe while she'd been miserably unhappy without him, he'd been frolicking in the sand on a tropical island with Molly.

Except that she didn't really think he was the frolicking type.

When he'd swallowed the last mouthful of beer,

Jake pulled his wallet out of his back pocket and set a ten-dollar bill on the bar beside the empty mug.

Her stomach tightened into painful knots as she braced herself to watch him push away from the bar and walk out the door.

She wanted to say something, but her throat was tight.

Her heart aching.

Was this really how it was going to be?

As if they were strangers all over again?

Courtney set her tray on the corner of the bar and read off her order pad: "I need a pint of Icky, a pitcher of Wild Horse with three glasses, a vodka martini, dirty, with two olives, and a Coke."

Sky busied herself getting the drinks.

She didn't look at the stool where Jake had been sitting, because she didn't want to watch him leave. Because she knew that it would rip her heart out of her chest again.

When Courtney's tray was loaded, she glanced down to the other end of the bar, to see if any of her other customers needed a refill.

Jake was still there.

Watching her.

She took a couple of steps in his direction, even as she cursed herself for being unable to stay away. When she was standing in front of him again, he placed a square velvet box on top of the money.

Sky just stared at it, her pulse racing.

She made no move to reach for the box, so Jake

opened the lid to reveal a square sapphire surrounded by diamonds and set on a platinum band.

The murmur of voices faded as the bar's other patrons abandoned their own conversations in favor of eavesdropping on the scene that was playing out before them.

Sky swallowed and tucked her hands into the front pockets of her jeans, resisting the urge to reach for the ring. "That's a heck of a tip."

"It's not a tip," Jake told her. "It's a proposal."

She looked at him then. "Is it?"

He nodded. "I know diamonds are traditional, but I thought the sapphire would suit you better."

"A proposal usually includes a question," Ellis Hagen pointed out from the other end of the bar.

"Sky knows I'm not good with words," Jake said.

And maybe she should snatch up the ring and the man, but after five weeks, she wanted more. She needed more. She needed to know that she mattered enough for him to make the effort.

"I think I deserve the words," she said to him now.

He nodded again. "You're right. You do. So how about if I start by telling you that I love you?"

She felt her throat tighten. "That's a pretty good start."

"A slow start, I'd say, if this is the first time you're saying the words," Gavin Virga chimed in.

Jake looked at Sky, his expression chagrined. "I obviously didn't think this through," he acknowledged. "Or I might have chosen a less public venue."

"But you're here now," Sky said, mentally crossing her fingers that he wouldn't walk out. "And the next round's on me if everyone else can shut up for five minutes and at least pretend to mind their own business."

"But this is so much more interesting," Doug Holland said.

Sky shot him a withering glance.

"Shutting up," he promised.

She turned back to Jake.

"It's true," he said to her now. "I love you. I don't know when or how it happened, but the more time I spent with you, the more I couldn't imagine my life without you. I didn't want to imagine a life without you in it.

"But I needed some time to get my life together before I could ask you to share it—because more than anything, what I want is to share my life with you. Because I love you, Sky, and I hope you still love me, too."

"I do," she confessed softly. "But I thought I'd freaked you out by telling you how I felt."

"What freaked me out was knowing how *I* felt," he confided. "Because I watched you with your family at the wedding, and I saw the closeness between you and your siblings, the way you dote on your nieces and nephews. And I knew you needed to be with someone who could give you a family of your own."

"What I need is to be with someone who loves me. And if, at some point down the road, we can work kids into that arrangement, that would be great. But if not, at least we'd be together."

"I want to give you everything you want," he said. "Everything you deserve. That's why I left."

"I'm confused," she admitted.

"You're not the only one," Jerry Tate remarked.

But Jake's gaze didn't shift from Sky's face. "I completed a thirty-day residential PTSD treatment program in Reno," he said, ignoring the other man's remark. "I needed to know that I could tackle my issues, to be worthy of you."

"You don't ever have to tackle anything on your own," Sky told him, coming around from behind the counter to take a seat beside him, wanting to ensure that this part of their conversation couldn't be overheard.

Though she would have liked to know where he was and what he was doing, she understood now why he'd kept that information to himself. That he'd probably had doubts, not just about the effectiveness of the program but his ability to stick with it.

And the realization that he'd not only sought treatment but completed a program brought on a whole new wave of emotions. Surprise. Gratitude. Happiness. Pride.

"How was it?" she asked gently.

"Brutal. Intense." He lifted his gaze to hers. "Life-changing."

"In a good way?" she asked cautiously.

"Yeah." He leaned closer and brushed his lips over hers in a gentle kiss. "In a very good way."

She smiled. "I'm glad."

"But I'm still a work in progress," he warned.

She knew that was true. She knew that he would likely battle the demons that haunted him for the rest of his life. But hopefully now he knew that he didn't have to battle alone. That if he let her, she'd gladly take up a sword and fight by his side—for Jake and their future together.

"I understand that you might not want to rush into setting a date or anything like that," he continued. "But I hope you'll at least agree to wear my ring on your finger, so you can look at it every day and know how much I love you even if I'm not always good at telling or showing you."

"You're doing just fine so far," she said, and held out her left hand.

"Is that a yes?"

"That's a very emphatic yes."

He removed the ring from the box and slid it on her third finger—to the accompaniment of cheers and applause around the room.

"Now kiss her," Ellis urged.

"Like you mean it this time," Gavin said.

Jake heeded their advice.

"What if I do want to rush into setting a date?" she asked, when he'd finally eased his lips from hers.

"You'd make me the happiest man in the world," he assured her.

"That's good," she said. "Because I don't want to wait to start the rest of my life with you. But there is one thing you might have to do first."

"Ask your father's permission?" he guessed.

"More like my sister's forgiveness," she said.

"I've already spoken to both of them," he told her.

Her brows lifted. "Before you came to see me?"

"I needed them in my corner in case I had to go to Plan B."

"What was Plan B?"

"Begging you to give me a second chance."

"I don't want you to beg," she said. "I just want you to love me."

"And I always will," he promised.

* * * * *

Look for Haylee Gilmore's story,
Meet Me Under the Mistletoe
*the next book in award-winning
author Brenda Harlen's miniseries
Match Made in Haven.*

*Coming in November 2020,
wherever Harlequin Special Edition
books and ebooks are sold.*

WE HOPE YOU ENJOYED
THIS BOOK FROM

Believe in love. Overcome obstacles. Find happiness.

Relate to finding comfort and strength in the
support of loved ones and enjoy the journey
no matter what life throws your way.

6 NEW BOOKS AVAILABLE EVERY MONTH!

COMING NEXT MONTH FROM

(H) HARLEQUIN
SPECIAL EDITION

Available August 18, 2020

#2785 THE MAVERICK'S BABY ARRANGEMENT
Montana Mavericks: What Happened to Beatrix?
by Kathy Douglass
In order to retain custody of his eight-month-old niece, Daniel Dubois convinces event planner and confirmed businesswoman Brittany Brandt to marry him. It's only supposed to be a mutually beneficial business agreement...*if* they can both keep their hearts out of the equation.

#2786 THE LAST MAN SHE EXPECTED
Welcome to Starlight • by Michelle Major
When Mara Reed agrees to partner with her sworn enemy, Parker Johnson, to help a close friend, she doesn't expect the feelings of love and tenderness that complicate every interaction with the handsome attorney. Will Mara and Parker risk everything for love?

#2787 CHANGING HIS PLANS
Gallant Lake Stories • by Jo McNally
Real estate developer Brittany Doyle is eager to bring the mountain town of Gallant Lake into the twenty-first century...by changing everything. Hardware store owner Nate Thomas hates change. These opposites refuse to compromise, except when it comes to falling in love.

#2788 A WINNING SEASON
Wickham Falls Weddings • by Rochelle Alers
When Sutton Reed returns to Wickham Falls after finishing a successful baseball career, he assumes he'll just join the family business and live an uneventful life. Until his neighbor's younger brother tries to steal his car, that is. Now he's finding himself mentoring the boy—and being drawn to Zoey Allen like no one else.

#2789 IN SERVICE OF LOVE
Sutter Creek, Montana • by Laurel Greer
Commitmentphobic veterinarian Maggie is focused on training a Great Dane as a service dog and expanding the family dog-training business. Can widowed single dad Asher's belief in love after loss inspire Maggie to risk her heart and find forever with the irresistible librarian?

#2790 THE SLOW BURN
Masterson, Texas • by Caro Carson
When firefighter Caden Sterling unexpectedly delivers Tana McKenna's baby by the side of the road, the unlikely threesome forms a special bond. Their flirty friendship slowly becomes more, until Tana's ex and the truth about her baby catches up with her. Can she win back the only man who can make this family complete?

**YOU CAN FIND MORE INFORMATION ON UPCOMING HARLEQUIN TITLES,
FREE EXCERPTS AND MORE AT HARLEQUIN.COM.**

HSECNM0820

SPECIAL EXCERPT FROM

⬧ HARLEQUIN

SPECIAL EDITION

*Real estate developer Brittany Doyle is eager to
bring the mountain town of Gallant Lake into the
twenty-first century...by changing everything.
Hardware store owner Nate Thomas hates change.
These opposites refuse to compromise, except when it
comes to falling in love.*

Read on for a sneak peek at
Changing His Plans,
*the next book in the Gallant Lake Stories
miniseries by Jo McNally.*

He stuck his head around the corner of the fasteners
aisle just in time to see a tall brunette stagger into the
revolving seed display. Some of the packets went flying,
but she managed to steady the display before the whole
thing toppled. He took in what probably had been a very
nice silk blouse and tailored trouser suit before she was
drenched in the storm raging outside. The heel on one of
the ridiculously high heels she was wearing had snapped
off, explaining why she was stumbling around.

"Having a bad morning?"

The woman looked up in annoyance, strands of dark,
wet hair falling across her face.

"You could say that. I don't suppose you have a shoe
repair place in this town?" She looked at the bright red
heel in her hand.

Nate shook his head as he approached her. "Nope. But hand it over. I'll see what I can do."

A perfectly shaped brow arched high. "Why? Are you going to cobble them back together with—" she gestured around widely "—maybe some staples or screws?"

"Technically, what you just described is the definition of cobbling, so yeah. I've got some glue that'll do the trick." He met her gaze calmly. "It'd be a lot easier to do if you'd take the shoe off. Unless you also think I'm a blacksmith?"

He was teasing her. Something about this soaking-wet woman still having so much…regal bearing…amused Nate. He wasn't usually a fan of the pearl-clutching country club set who strutted through Gallant Lake on the weekends and referred to his family's hardware store as "adorable." But he couldn't help admiring this woman's ability to hold on to her superiority while looking like she accidentally went to a water park instead of the business meeting she was dressed for. To be honest, he also admired the figure that expensive red suit was clinging to as it dripped water on his floor.

He held out his hand. "I'm Nate Thomas. This is my store."

She let out an irritated sigh. "Brittany Doyle." She slid her long, slender hand into his and gripped with surprising strength. He held it for just a half second longer than necessary before shaking off the odd current of interest she invoked in him.

Don't miss
Changing His Plans *by Jo McNally,*
available September 2020 wherever
Harlequin Special Edition books and ebooks are sold.

Harlequin.com